COUNTDOWN . . .

"Good afternoon to you, Mr. Griggs. Question: What of importance to the government is happening this Sunday?"

Dan's end of the line went silent for a moment, and Mark could imagine Dan scanning his advance calendar. "Mark, not a damn thing that I know about."

"That's the problem—we don't know about it. Something big is going to happen, and it won't be good. It has something to do with the communications industry, and the only thing I can come up with is that some attempt will be made to black out the communications network for the entire nation. If I were you, I'd have the armed forces crank up some kind of surprise alert for this weekend, something to keep their radio emergency network alive and working as well as it can. The Autovon is going to be shot all to hell if this blackout hits the phone system."

Time—that was Mark's biggest enemy now. Time. Friday, 11:00 A.M. A day and a half to Sunday. . . .

THE PENETRATOR SERIES:

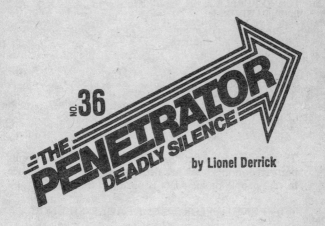

NO. 36

THE PENETRATOR

DEADLY SILENCE

by Lionel Derrick

PINNACLE BOOKS   LOS ANGELES

THE PENETRATOR #36: DEADLY SILENCE

Copyright © 1980 by Pinnacle Books

An original Pinnacle Books edition, published for the first time anywhere.

First printing, June 1980

ISBN: 0-523-40673-8

Special acknowledgment to Chet Cunningham

Cover illustration by George Wilson

Printed in the United States of America

PINNACLE BOOKS, INC.
2029 Century Park East
Los Angeles, California 90067

Anger is the genesis of frustration, but when such frustration begets violence, corrective action must take place, and then the cool logic of reasonable men will prevail with pragmatic authority once again leading the masses.

JASON EDWIN MARLOWE

CONTENTS

DEADLY SILENCE

PROLOGUE

Mark Hardin is the Penetrator.

For more years than he cared to remember he had been a one-man force fighting for justice, for the underdog, for the little guy who could not afford a battery of lawyers and an appeal to the U.S. Supreme Court—for the victims. The Penetrator has no government agency behind him, no clout, no huge budget or free transportation in government jets or with the armed forces.

The Penetrator does it alone.

He goes wherever he finds injustice and the downtrodden, and he makes some changes.

Every hoodlum in America and in a number of other countries around the world have to reckon with the Penetrator, because he just might pop onto the scene and disrupt a lot of well-conceived criminal plans. It was a factor: they had to think about it, and it slowed down a lot of them.

Mark Hardin tried not to dwell on the past. He

knew his history well enough. But some of the Penetrator-watchers could recite almost every strike he had made against crime once he threw in with the common man.

Mark was a patriotic American and proud of it. He did not run off to Canada, criminally violating American draft laws. Instead he volunteered and served in Vietnam during the terrible days when his life was on the line for months at a time.

When he came home he was discharged before either his mind or his body had been totally healed. As he recovered at a friend's desert hideaway in California, mobsters killed the girl whom he had grown to love, and that started it all. He went after the killers with a total vengeance learned in the heat of combat. Mark riddled the Mafia "family" in Los Angeles, took from them nearly half a million dollars in unreturnable money that had been part of a heroin buy, and slowly realized that he had found his new cause. He would track down killers and evil-doers, manipulators, criminals of every type that the regular law-enforcement channels were having trouble with, or couldn't touch.

So began his one-man crusade that had spanned several years and some thirty-six individual engagements. Still the battle wasn't even won, let alone the war. Each day in the communications room he found a new target that he should be dealing with. But he had only so much time—and energy.

He operated from the desert hideaway: a specially constructed residence in a borax mine in the mountains near Barstow, California. The whole complex was built in the tunnels and vaulted rooms of the worked-out mine. From the surface it was impossible to tell the hideaway was there. It had its own water supply, electric generator, and air conditioning and heating plants. Since it was underground, heating and cooling presented few problems even in the desert. Rock hounds and hikers had walked directly across the Stronghold and never knew it.

But inside the occupants were aware of the strangers. A fence constructed of small audio sensors ringed the Stronghold and could be so finely tuned that a running coyote would set them off and transmit a silent signal to a light and beeper inside the communications room.

Mark Hardin had killed. He had learned the fine art of killing humans when in the army and practiced the techniques in his Vietnam days, and now he killed only when he had to, and never from anger or vengeance, but only dispassionately and when it seemed mandatory.

His reverence for life had been deepened when an old Indian at the Stronghold explained that Mark was part Indian; then he traced his parents back through his orphan years to find that he was half Cheyenne. Next David Red Eagle, a Cheyenne medicine chief, began teaching Mark the old ways, drilling him in the ancient Indian arts of tracking, of hunting with bow and arrow, of living off the land, of going long distances through the desert with only the aid of his two feet and a mind conditioned to withstand the pain, the heat, the lack of food and water.

David Red Eagle had taught Mark much more. He insisted that Mark eat more meat, cooked lightly in the Indian fashion. He indoctrinated Mark into the ancient art of *sho-tu-ca*, the secrets of the Cheyenne Dog Soldiers who were such fierce warriors. With the ancient arts and admixtures of modern day psychology, the *sho-tu-ca* became a powerful tool the Penetrator could use to help overcome his opponents.

Mark had been trained by the army in the use of

all of its hand weapons, and his skill with each quickly surpassed that of the army instructors.

Because of his exploits against criminals, Mark was a wanted criminal himself, and on many states' most-wanted list. Still he *never* took a life unless he had to, never killed in anger, and never fired in the presence of any lawfully constituted police authorities. He had broken that rule only once, in Seattle, where a band of police had taken matters in their own hands and formed themselves into a burglars' ring and then a killers-for-hire mob which Mark broke up.

Mark was a powerfully built man somewhere between thirty and thirty-five, and carrying his two hundred and five pounds easily on a broad-shouldered, heavily muscled, six-foot-two-inch frame.

With black hair and eyebrows and the dark, intelligently glittering eyes beneath them, his complexion was a shade darker than .white from his half-Indian blood. He tanned to a coppery brown when he got enough sun. His hawkbill nose and high cheekbones tended to reveal his half-Cheyenne ancestry. They all gave his face, even in repose, a smoldering, critical expression. When he frowned, a cold, deadly aura came through that stemmed from his dedication to his duty.

When moving, Mark had the supple litheness of a young cougar, with a lean, hungry look of a top-conditioned athlete. He spoke little, using language when it served his purpose. His accent was American, CBS news neutral, but critical listeners might detect a slight Far West twang if they paid attention. Many times his opposition seldom had time to peg his voice before they were either captured or dead.

In all his missions, Mark had made few lasting friendships. This was deliberately calculated after one young girl who simply said hello to him one afternoon became a pawn used against him, and as a

4

result the hoodlums killed her. So Now Mark pulled back from lasting entanglements. That served another purpose as well. No one knew for sure who the Penetrator was. Only eight persons alive were aware of who he was and how to contact him, and they were true and loyal friends who would protect him.

Now, as he jogged along in the California desert, Mark thought of the status board in the Stronghold. That was usually a sign that he was rested and anxious to get started on a new mission.

He could remember nothing that seemed especially urgent. There had been a rash of seemingly unrelated walkouts and slowdowns in the communications field lately, but it could be that it was just time for the unions to go in for a new contract. He would watch it.

In the trail ahead he saw a rattlesnake sunning itself on a long slab of rock. He ran around it and the snake hardly noticed the strange being passing. Mark tried to think of some Indian saying that would cover the situation, but couldn't, so he turned and headed back for the Stronghold. He was eager now to take another look at the status board and see what new the professor had added.

The professor was Dr. Willard Haskins, former geology professor at USC, and now retired. He had built the Stronghold and asked Mark to come recuperate there after his Vietnam tour. They hit it off and he stayed on. Now they had a friendship so strong nothing could even dent it.

The three of them, Mark, Red Eagle, and the professor made a powerful team, one that would fight crime wherever they found it.

Mark picked up the pace again as he saw the outline of the right bluff ahead and reached out with more speed for the last half mile.

Chapter 1

SABOTAGE FROM THE RANKS

CHICAGO, AUGUST 3

Arnold Spivack was mad as hell. He was mad at almost everyone as he left his apartment to go to work at Chicago's Fifteenth Street master switching station of the giant Illinois Bell telephone system. In the first place he had a screaming-yelling name-calling fight with his live-in girl friend last night, and she threatened again to pull out and leave him. His left heel still hurt where he bruised it playing racket ball; then this morning Larson, the damn business agent of his union local, got him out of bed and said he had a special job for him, but he had to show up at a parking lot at a bar down the block from the switching station a half hour before he usually reported to work.

That whistle-blowing union punk Larson was what made him the maddest of all. But Larson said it could be worth some big bucks if it all went right. Just the meeting and one little errand. Larson wouldn't ask him to kill anybody, not his style, but Spivack knew damn well that it wouldn't be anything legal either—not with that fucking Larson mixed up in it.

Spivack shrugged. Even if he got a couple hundred it was good money, and he could use the extra. He drove past the regular company parking lot and swung in at the side of a closed bar on the corner of Twenty-ninth Street. The black Caddy Larson always drove sat right where the guy said it would. The windows were rolled up and the motor running.

Spivack parked beside the Caddy and turned off his engine. As he got out of his car the Cadillac's front door opened, and Spivack slid into the soft-seat luxury of the big car.

Larson was grinning his perfect capped-tooth grin that always made Spivack frown.

"Yeah, I'm here, Larson. What the hell you want?"

Larson, a small, neatly dressed man, carefully shaved and wearing some kind of cologne, shook his head. His suit was expensive and fit perfectly:

"What's this tough-guy bit, Spivack. I pull you out of the gutter and get you off welfare and on a good job paying big bucks and I get the sneer and the 'what the hell you want' routine?"

"Sorry Larson, but I had a bad night." He looked at the small man and waited.

"I've got an important job I want you to do for me, for the union. You work at the E.S.S. at Twenty-ninth, right?"

"Yeah, the Electronic Switching System."

"How many phones does that control?"

"About sixty thousand, give or take a thousand depending on installations and stops that day."

"Good, just right. I understand it has lots of backup systems, and you're one of the guys who

8

works on the mechanical monster when it needs some delicate rerouting or for overloads, problems, breakdowns, that sort of thing."

"Yeah, so?"

"I'm getting there, Spivack, just relax. I want you to figure out some way to blow the whole sixty thousand phones off the air all at once for ten hours."

"Christ, all sixty thousand? Why me?"

"Because you're a good man I can trust. You've had enough combat experience in 'Nam so I know you won't be afraid to do it. And I figure it's time you need a little thrill in your humdrum life. This order came down from the top, and I don't want anything going wrong. Figure out how you're going to do it, then call me at the office and we'll get together on the timing. We've got two days to put it all together."

"I spend all day keeping that thing working, now you want me to zap it?"

"Yeah, Spivack. Now I want you to blow it off the system for ten hours. It isn't my idea, Spivack, the orders come from the national, so don't get your nose out of joint. You follow orders the same way I do. Just figure out how to do it, and then we blow it."

"I'll have some expenses," Spivack said starting to get an idea.

"How much?"

"I need to take care of a guy, at a national guard armory. Two fifty for him, a thousand for me. I'm putting my tail on the line here, Larson."

"Okay, they expected that; it's worth it to them. Don't ask me why. Hell *I* don't know why. They yell at me, and I come talk with the best man I got. Meet me here tomorrow morning instead of calling. I don't want anything that can be traced or tapped."

"Me too," Spivack said. "I ain't about to get my

tail in a wringer for no thousand clams. You be careful and I'll be damned careful."

Larson nodded and they split up. Spivack went on to work; he sat in the parking lot for ten minutes so he wouldn't be too early. He didn't want to attract any attention. He was getting to enjoy his work at the E.S.S. Someday he'd be the cat up there at the M.C.C., the Master Control Center panel. He'd put on the headset and he could plug into any of the dozens of trunk groups leaving the center for Class 4 tandem offices, from which routes could be made to Class 3 primary centers, and down to Class 2 toll centers, and then right down to Class 1 regional centers. There were only ten regional centers in the whole country. All of this pyramidal system came up from a base of thousands of Class 5 end offices where the householder's first line entered the great switching network. It was all there right at the M.C.C. and it carried with it a type of power that Spivack could only imagine.

He worried about the Electronic Switching System because it had one built-in function he didn't know enough about. The damn thing talked to the operator through a teletypewriter. You asked it a question and it gave you the answer, or it told you if something was wrong, or might go wrong. The system constantly ran checks on itself, like a hypochondriac constantly looking for something to worry about, or for a condition that could overload or blow out a section. How was he going to get around that? It did much more than troubleshoot, including the checking of each telephone it served and asking it six times a second if it needed a dial tone. If somebody picked up a phone it usually had a dial tone before the handset reached the user's ear.

So how could he get around all the built-in safeguards? He thought about it all day, and decided his first gut reaction was right. His buddy in the national guard would be the key, and it would be explosives and fire in one of the master control rooms, where all the black boxes were that made the whole system work.

There was no way he could make it look like an accident. It would have to be sabotage, so he should make it a good one. He wasn't exactly sure how yet, but his army buddy would help. As he figured it, there were about a hundred and twenty people working in the Fourteenth Street facility. Everyone would be a suspect, including him, but there was no other way. He had no gripe with the company, no record of problems or discontent. They'd never suspect him. It had to be.

Three days later he was all set. Ten minutes after his shift ended at 5:00 P.M., Spivack slid into the computer master control room and set down a five gallon can of gasoline, then tipped it over so the fuel spilled out. He pulled the pins on two white phosphorous grenades and held the spoons down. At the door he stepped outside, then tossed the two grenades at the can of gasoline and slammed the heavy steel door and felt it lock. He never even heard the explosion. The steel door of the computer room was designed to withstand fire and explosions from the outside.

Spivack carried his lunch pail as usual and walked out the side door and down half a block to where he had moved his car at lunchtime. He was out of the complex before he heard the fire alarm from inside. He drove away slowly so he wouldn't attract attention. Three blocks away he stopped and took off the old license plates from a wrecked car that Larson had provided him. He'd fastened the phony ones over his own with rubber bands. He threw them in the alley garbage can, got back in and drove home, his radio set to an all-news station.

11

The news flash came before he got to his apartment.

"An explosion and fire less than fifteen minutes ago, ripped through the master control computer room at the Fourteenth Street master switching station of Illinois Bell, and has put at least sixty thousand telephones in the central area of Chicago out of service.

"A company spokesman said rerouting and repair work has started already, but the massive damage done to the complicated computer switching system may take more than twenty-four hours to repair. The company spokesman said that the explosion was not 'of an electrical nature.' He said they did not know what caused the problem but the fire marshal as well as police and arson squads were investigating.

"A company employee on the scene told one of our reporters at the fire that he had smelled gasoline just after the explosion. Another employee said the door to the switching control room was blown off and the entire area was filled with the most dense white smoke that he could ever remember seeing. He could compare it only with white phosphorous grenades and mortar rounds the army uses. The official company spokesperson will not speculate what caused the explosion or if it were accidental or deliberate."

Arnold Spivack turned off the radio and laughed. Damn but that WP must have done a job on those microcircuits and fancy black boxes in the computer area. Spivack didn't have a question about why or what it might be a larger part of. He simply didn't worry about it. He had a more pressing problem. What kind of present was he going to buy his woman to keep her happy?

Marve Butler held the phone and glared at the instrument. "What the hell you mean, set up a walkout for the sixth? No way. I've got a binding contract, the companies are happy, the men are happy, I'm getting new members all the time. Nobody wants to go out, let alone break the contract. You're off your gourd, man. Who the hell are you, anyway?"

The voice on the other end was ultimately calm, poised, and forceful. It gave Marve Butler a small chill.

"You don't really have to know who I am, Mr. Butler. The point is that the National Communications Council, of which your union is a member, is in delicate negotiations at this very moment, and we have decided that it will be for the good of organized labor in general, and our national union and your local in particular, if we have a show of force on August Sixth. We're looking for your solidarity, for your cooperation in this important matter."

"Is that right? What vital matter? Tell me about it."

"I'm afraid I'm not authorized to do that."

"Well get somebody the fuck over here who is authorized to do that. I don't answer to you, hotshot. I answer only my union members."

"Mr. Butler, I assure you this is a vital matter, and in the interests of union solidarity. I'm asking you again to cooperate."

"Look, fish face! I don't have the slightest idea who the hell you are. I only heard of this National Communications Council outfit once, and it sounded like a pretty raunchy outfit. I'm running one of the biggest goddamned unions in Hollywood, and if you think I'm gonna shut down forty studios, twenty radio stations, and ten TV stations because of just one shitty phone call like this, you're strictly dumbass.

Now, you get somebody on the line I know, and I'll consider your request. Otherwise just shut up and get off my phone."

"Mr. Butler, you sound like a dedicated union man; just be sure you're dedicated to the right side. Now, why don't I have one of our Los Angeles executives come to see you. He'll show you his credentials and letters from your national headquarters. Then I'm sure we can work out something."

"Yeah, big shot. You just do that. But I won't hold my breath." Butler tossed the phone on the hook and slapped the table with the palm of his hand. As if he didn't have enough problems with the goddamned runaway productions, now this son of a bitch had to get on his back. Pull everyone out for a day? Ridiculous. Unthinkable. He had good control over his people and he wasn't going to mess it up for some hotshot in Chicago. Probably political anyway.

Marve went back to his list. Topping it off was a beef out at Universal. His man had struck out there yesterday. He'd have to get over there and talk to the people involved and see if he could get it straightened out. He had almost fifteen hundred people working at Universal right now, which was going like a bat out of hell with all those TV movies, and series, and the feature films. The place was humming again. What Hollywood needed was ten studios like Universal. Then they wouldn't be running off to San Diego, and Monaco, and Pawtucket, Rhode Island, to make movies and even shoot series.

His phone buzzed.

Marve answered, his eyes still on the clipboard list. "Yeah, Betsy."

"Mr. Butler, I've got a Nate Tausch on one. He said it was important."

"Everything's important, put him on."

14

The connection clicked. "Yes, Mr. Tausch, Butler here. What can I do for you?"

"Mr. Butler, I'm from the National Communications Council and my national president just called and said I should set up a meeting with you. Could I come over in half an hour?"

"This some more of that bullshit about my pulling my men off the job in two days?"

"Yes, Mr. Butler. It's a vital part of a campaign we're on and I'm sure you'll want to know all the details and how this one strike can do so much for the communications union all over the country."

"Well, hell. I was supposed to be out at Universal this morning, but I guess if you make it fast I can work you in. You be here by ten-thirty, right?"

"Yes, of course, Mr. Butler. I'll see you shortly."

Marve Butler hung up and sighed. A half hour and he'd tear to pieces whomever they sent over, then he'd go to Universal. He went to the office door, opened it, and stared at his secretary. Marve's wife had hired her. His Italian wife insisted on picking out his secretary because the last one had been too pretty. Betsy wasn't pretty at all, plain in fact was what Marve's wife had called her. But she had other qualities.

"Betsy, come in here and don't bring your book."

Betsy was twenty-four, twenty-five pounds overweight for her five-four frame, she wore glasses and slightly out of date fashions. But Betsy was an excellent typist, took shorthand, and had a fine telephone voice. She was eager to learn. So far Marve had taken her as a fucking virgin and taught her everything he knew about sex. It had been a remarkable year. His wife never had a glimmer.

"Yes, Mr. Butler?" she said once inside his office.

"Betsy, lock the front door and turn out the lights, then get yourself back in here."

Betsy smiled and hurried to the front door. She

15

was back almost at once and stood in front of him.

"You want to have a little fun today, Betsy? I've got twenty minutes to kill, so why don't we mess around a little." He pushed his hand down the front of her blouse and was pleased he had at last talked her into leaving her bra at home.

Betsy giggled and reached for his crotch, rubbing the hardness that extended upward toward his belt.

A half hour later Marve Butler had sent Betsy out for doughnuts and told her to take a break and be back at eleven. He didn't want her in the office in case he had to get rough with the visitor. Marve checked in his drawer, took out a five-inch switchblade and a pair of brass knuckles. He'd won the kunckles in a crap game in Jersey City years ago. He was ready.

Marve left his office door open so he could hear the knock on the outer one. It came five minutes later. He went to the front and opened the door.

"Mr. Butler?" a small dark man said. He wore an expensive suit and had a beard that probably had been shaved two hours ago but looked razor-ready again. "I hope I'm not too late. Actually this won't take but a few minutes."

Marve backed into the office. "Come in."

The man walked in and looked at the empty desk. "Is your secretary out? She has such a fine telephone voice."

"Yes, she's on an errand, she won't bother us. We can talk privately in the other room."

As he said it another man came through the outer door and closed it solidly. Marve Butler knew right then he had made a mistake. The other man was at least six-four and heavy and a scowl looked as fixed on his face as the pistol he held in his right hand. Too late, Marve saw that it was a .22 High Standard with a silencer attached.

"Hey, why the gun?" Marve asked.

"Oh, that," the small man said. "That's our credentials, Mr. Butler. We didn't want any misunderstandings. Into the other office."

"Hey, what's to misunderstand? Our union is a member of the team; we do our share." They walked into the inner office and the big man closed the door. When the gunman's back was half turned, Marve whipped out the switchblade and snicked it open. His left arm snaked around the small man's neck and the blade touched his throat.

"Don't turn around, big man!" Marve bellowed. "You do and your buddy here gets his throat sliced open from ear to ear. You read me?"

"Yeah. I hear you." For a second he froze, then the enforcer spun on one foot, his finger squeezing the trigger. The first silent round missed. In a flash of a second Marve knew he was going to die, and he was determined to take one of them with him. He plunged the sharp blade into the small man's throat, just as the next bullet from the .22 whispered into his shoulder. The pain brought a scream from Marve and he jerked his right hand sideways, the blade in his hand slashed through the windpipe and the second carotid artery and out the side of the small man's neck.

The body in front of Marve started to fall. The gunman lifted his sights and put three .22 long rifle rounds from the silenced weapon into Marve's face. One splattered his right eye as it bored into Marve's brain. A second took off a chunk of his nose and slanted downward into his mouth. The third round blasted through his forehead into his cerebellum, shattering it into a dozen fragments, pulping that section of the late Marvin Butler's brain even as he died from the round through his eye.

The gunman's name was Al, and now he stared in disgust at all the blood pouring from his former boss's throat. He never used a blade, too much mess to clean up. Now he screwed the silencer off the High Standard, slid it into a special holder in his jacket, and then pushed the High Standard into its holster. He went quickly into the hall and brought back two large plastic bags. The army called them body bags. As quickly as he could he stuffed the bloody body of his partner into the first bag and zipped it up. Then he pushed Marve's bulkier form into the second bag.

He unwrapped two towels from his waist and mopped himself and the blood on the floor. Then he took some water from the coffee machine and carefully cleaned the rest of the blood off the linoleum floor. When he was satisfied with the job he stuffed the two towels into the bag with the smaller body, than carried it down the hall to the back stairs and out to a small van he had parked at the rear entrance. Nobody asked him what he was doing. He saw no one on his trip.

When he went back to the office he taped a message on the door, then picked up Marve's body bag, took it out, pushed the door closed, and headed for the stairs. He met a salesman in the hall, but the man didn't even look up. He seemed to have enough problems of his own.

The enforcer was halfway to the stairs when he heard someone behind him. He turned and saw a girl stop and look at the note on the door. She wasn't a very tall girl and she was plain as a whitewashed barn.

Besty stood reading the note taped to the door of Local 452.

"Betsy: I'm going out of town for two weeks. The International will send over a man to hold down the fort for us. I have some personal business, no big deal, so don't worry. Oh, that guy who called and said he was coming over never showed. Sorry I had

18

to leave so fast. You can close up the office and take the rest of the day off. The new guy will be here tomorrow. Watch out for yourself. Marve."

The note wasn't signed. She pulled it down, opened the door with her key, and went inside. Everything was normal. She looked inside his office and saw that Marve's briefcase was still on his desk. If it were personal business he wouldn't take the case. She sniffed and thought she smelled a strange odor, but decided it didn't mean a thing. Her nose was seldom right about smells anyway.

Betsy turned off the lights, locked the door, and went home. Anytime she could get half a day off from this outfit she was going to take it!

BIG SANDY, WYOMING, AUGUST 6

The sun had come out about two that afternoon and now warmed Walton Jamison as he slid along the powder over the heavy ice pack that was now covered with twelve to fourteen feet of snow. "A base of fourteen feet with six inches of powder," he could just hear the ski report now. His cross-country skis slapped ahead as he moved up a short incline. Jamison paused on the crest and looked ahead. Wind River Peak rose beyond. He had another mile, perhaps two, before he came to the shoulder of the 13,225 foot Rocky Mountain peak where the microwave relay station sat.

He had not really known that ninety to ninety-five percent of all long-distance calls across the country went by microwave at least part of the way. Most of them went all the way by microwave, the electronic impulses shot from one line-of-sight relay station to the next, skipping across the width of the continent in only a few seconds.

He wiped sweat from his forehead, realized that it hadn't frozen there, and smiled. It was warmer than he had expected. But when the sun went down and the wind picked up it would be cold. He had to be done and heading back long before then.

Jamison adjusted the pack on his back and moved out again, slanting upward toward the relay station in the swift, measured strides a long-distance skier needed when moving up a hill.

His digital watch showed that it was just after three when he slanted down the short run and came to the tower itself. It had been brought preassembled by a huge helicopter, and it had taken a week of effort to get it set in place. The choppers had coughed and sputtered in the thin air, and the devil winds whipped and gusted first one way and then another over the mountain. Several chopper pilots gave up and went home.

The phone company figured on servicing the tower by small helicopter once it was put in. But they had to reevaluate. They at last got the station planted and finished, then decided they would send in a ground team from Big Sandy when servicing work was needed.

Jamison took off his skis and leaned them against the steel beams of the tower. They took no chances with forest fires burning down a wooden tower. The snow came up nearly halfway on the tower, but the small cabin and electronic assembly still sat fifteen feet off the snow. He checked it again, making doubly certain where he would place the charges, then went to work.

Jamison put charges on each of the microwave senders and receivers, working slowly, carefully. There could be no mistakes. He worked with the confidence of long practice around explosives. When he was done he inserted electric taps, attaching them to a long lead that trailed fifty yards down the slope. Jamison took his skis, his pack, his gloves, and the magneto and went to the end of the wire and hooked up the contacts.

He looked up at the tower and its bell-like pickup antennas. It made a pretty sight against the blue sky, in the crisp mountain air, with a scattering of light white clouds.

He twisted the magneto and saw the explosions go off in perfect unison. Jamison ducked as debris scattered nearby. The fire began at once where he had left the can of gasoline. By the time a spotter plane could fly over to look at the smoke, the tower house would be burned to ashes and the destruction of the relay station would be complete.

Jamison pulled down all of the detonation wire he could recover and stuffed it into his pack with the magneto. He would discard them both well down the trail. Once more he dug into the pack and checked a can of beer. It was nicely chilled, so he drank it.

Then he slid into his ski bindings, put his pack on and moved out toward home. Now all he needed was a good sharp wind to wipe out his tracks or an inch of snowfall, and then all evidence of his trail would be gone forever.

Jamison made good time now, slanting through the glistening crystals of snow, back down toward the timberline where he would have some protection in case a jet raced out to discover why the microwave had gone dead. He stopped part way down and put on his snow-white windbreaker and his white overpants. Even the tops of his skis had been painted white, and now it would take an eagle's keen eye to spot him on the white slopes, even by someone in a slow-moving plane. All he would have to do was stay still in the snow and a man in a plane a hundred feet away probably would look right over him and not realize he was there.

Jamison laughed, thinking about the other half of the money. He remembered what his college coach had told him: get out of skiing and back into football where some real money could be earned after graduation.

Hey, fifteen thousand for one day's work wasn't bad, not bad at all. He'd never before seen the guy who offered him the cash. He showed up one day at the bar in Big Sandy and said he wanted to talk. There aren't that many strangers in Big Sandy, and before the afternoon was over, Jamison had the job. He didn't know who the man was, or why he wanted the tower blown, and frankly, Jamison didn't give a damn.

Chapter 2

FUN TIME IN PHOENIX

Victor Jerele sat in a small room in his air-conditioned house in Phoenix before a six-foot-wide map of the United States. It had been put together carefully and showed all major cities and states, the telegraph and telephone trunklines, microwave relay routes, major newspapers, and the entire TV network system. The board was glowing with several colored lights, each signifying a separate system, wire, microwave, newspaper, or TV.

Jerele was a short man, five-feet-two inches tall, and he carried a hundred and eighty pounds. He had a headful of blond hair now grown a little long, and thick-lensed glasses which he constantly adjusted as they slipped down on his nose. One earpiece was held in place with a pin through the connecting hole where a screw had fallen out six months ago.

Jerele had gray eyes, fat cheeks, and a small nose. He boasted perfect teeth and tended them like shining jewels. Three of his front teeth had been capped as soon as he could afford it. Now he combed fingers through his long hair in anticipation as he sat down in the oversized swivel chair in front of the board.

"It won't be long now," Jerele said to no one. He looked at the display and at a clipboard in his hand listing the various light switches and which one each controlled.

A small speaker over the map came on.

"Mr. Jerele, we're getting the first report now. We have a total disruption of over sixty thousand phones in Chicago. A total wipeout, with reports that it will be up to a week before all of the damage can be repaired and the lines back in operation."

"Delightful!" Jerele said to the speaker, who couldn't hear him, and reached to the board and turned off switch No. 73 which blacked out a large area around Chicago. The rest of the board twinkled and glowed with almost a hundred lights.

Victor Jerele had waited a long time for this moment. He had worked up through the ranks in the communications unions, in the CWA, and he had fought hard. The first time he had been elected president in Minneapolis it had been an education. He thought unions elected presidents by votes. He chuckled now. It had been a bloody knockdown and knuckle-busting affair. When the smoke cleared and the ambulances were gone, they voted again. About half moved up to vote this time, and only those who had the pink ballots with Victor's name on them were allowed to get anywhere near the front of the auditorium where the ballot boxes were. It was a closed meeting of course, and nobody talked, and Victor Jerele found himself the "compromise" candidate of the CWA in Minneapolis, because he had recruited the biggest, toughest, and meanest sons of bitches he could find in the ranks to be his bodyguards.

After the first group of fights, there was no opposition. He could still remember the body count. Three concussions from blunt instruments (pipes); two broken arms from heavy falling objects (CWA member in boots); twelve bloody noses (fists, elbows, knees); and twenty-four men with lacerations, cuts, and bruises (fists, feet, and teeth). All in all it had been a heady feeling to be in charge of all that power. He held it for almost ten years.

Then he came to the point where he wanted to move up in the national and he did, but he was there only a short time and made a bigger deal. Now here he was, watching the experiment that could put him on the road to being the most powerful union man in the world! He was president of the National Communications Council of America. And it had brought all of the communications unions into one giant, massive, and all-powerful alliance, while not violating the law in any sense. They were "cooperating," not acting in concert, which his lawyers told him made all the difference.

The front had grown like a watermelon vine on a hot day in Texas. Now he had this small test, to see just how much muscle he had built into his group in the last three years. He had to see how quickly he could shut down the entire communications system for two hundred twenty-five million people. Shut it off cold, wipe out network TV and radio, squeeze newspapers down to local news, turn off the spigot of communications to an in-city trickle. All that would be left would be ham radio operators, a little bit of military radio, and the good old citizen's band good buddy broadcast!

"Mr. Jerele," the speaker said. "Confirmation on the tower of the Bell system microwave relay on Wind River Peak. The microwave system went down for two hours before they switched to an alter-

25

nate route they had as backup around that particularly remote station."

"Hot damn! That's as good as a winner for us. Two hours is what we ultimately need," Jerele said out loud to no one again. He picked up a phone and pushed a button, then touched the ring switch twice.

"Yeah?" a woman's soft voice said.

"Mello, if you're not busy, I'd like you to come into the map room for a while."

"Well, I'm doing my nails."

"Forget the nails and get your little round ass in here!" Jerele felt his lips quiver as he shouted into the instrument, then slammed it down. That goddamned woman was going to have to go. If she wasn't so damned cute he'd stash her in a minute.

He sat there watching the lights, then he flipped switch No. 42 that blacked out the national TV radio network over the Northwest and North Central States. Over twenty percent of all network traffic went through that one Rocky Mountain relay. He'd have to cut the other feeds to the South and Midwest and Southwest before he could blank out all the TV nets, but he could do it. Enough men with enough dynamite could do almost anything.

Mello Tone came into the room. She paused at the door a moment and posed for him in her bikini, like the model she had once been, and then slammed the door.

"Gawd, but it's dark in here," she said.

"Mello, don't say 'Gawd.' It simply broadcasts the fact to everyone listening that you came out of the gutter."

"Who the hell cares?"

"I care. You should care. Come here."

She went to him, stood beside him and his board.

"You still messing around with this jerk-off toy of yours?"

"It's no toy, Mello, it's a display board and shows

26

the progress of a project I'm working on. It demonstrates my ability to do the job I was hired to do. See those dark areas? Those have been blacked out; they get no network news on radio or TV, no telephone calls, long distance, no news wire, no telegrams, no TV shows at all."

"Wow, that's really hot shit. Who gives a fuck?"

"Mello, that's no way for a lady to talk." He shook his head and took hold of her wrist. "Am I going to have to punish you again?"

"Sure, spank me again. Please spank me!"

Jerele laughed. She always could get around him. She was wild and unpredictable, a child with a woman's body who left him with a hard-on half the time.

"Soon, little savage. But not quite yet, the experiment is still on."

"Mr. Jerele," the speaker overhead said. "Word just in that the microwave feed through Atlanta to the whole Southeast has been cut."

"Good, good." He reached over and flipped another switch on the small control board in front of him; the Southeast blacked out. His hand covered the girl's right breast and he squeezed it gently.

"See, Mello, see how it's working? When all the lights on the board go off, the project will be completed."

She didn't move his hand, instead she snuggled closer to him.

"But you said this was just a test."

"True, small wise one, true." He leaned over and kissed the soft flatness of her bare stomach. "Now it is practice, but soon the real game comes, and I have to know if I'm ready."

She frowned at him, her small round face twisted, hands on her hips. "Vic, did you have a shower this morning? You smell like a goddamned pig."

27

He hit her, his fist thumped into the same place he had just kissed and she winced, then laughed.

"You've got chicken guts for muscles, Vic, you know that? Your bed action ain't bad, but the rest of you is pig fat and ugly. Why don't you skinny down a little?" She jumped out of hitting range and laughed at him. "Vic, I gotta go have a shower. I try to stay clean in this bake oven, know what I mean? You get tired of playing with your toy, stop in and scrub my front."

Victor Jerele shook his head and sighed. She was an enigma to him, an absolute puzzle. Sometimes for a day or so he thought he was making progress with her; then she reverted to her gutter language and her four showers a day and her delightful bawdy, sexy, whore-ready behavior that left him confused and sexually aroused.

The speaker pulled him back to the work.

"Word that the problem in Hollywood is solved. A new temporary union leader is in power at the helm and says he can order his men and women off the shows originating from Hollywood on a two-shift notice."

"Thank you!" With delight Vic flipped the switch cutting the West Coast TV feed from Hollywood, then leaned back. That was the end of his test. Yes, it would work. Yes, he had the clout to make it work on the grass roots level and black out at least ninety-five percent of the nation for a two-to-four-hour period.

"Boss," the speaker toned. "We got somebody on the wire here, line one, and he's just mad as pure hell. Says he's from the headquarters of the AFL-CIO and he wants to talk to you just hog slippery fast."

"Headquarters? Damn AFL-CIO headquarters, huh? I'll be damned. Must have stepped on some toes. I'll take it."

He picked up the phone, punched line one and leaned back in the big soft chair.

"Yes, hello. This is Victor Jerele, president of the Communications Council of America. Whom am I speaking to?"

"Mr. Jerele, this is Hank Adams. I work with Mr. Wilson and he is just mad as hell. I finally talked him into letting me call you instead of him. He's burning over the fracas out in Hollywood with CWA Local 452. What can you tell me to calm him down?"

"Mr. Adams, I don't think you understand our position. Our group here is an overhead advisory consortium. We're in the business of setting up plans and procedures for massive action in our industry so we can make massive gains for our members."

"Mr. Jerele. Cut the bullshit. I know exactly what your group is. I was in on the planning. I sat in with you and George well into the program. Don't give me your public relations line of shit. What did you do out there with CWA 452?"

"The kid gloves are off. Okay, Adams. You must be George's new hatchet man. I'll give it to you straight. Your man at 452 is an old-fashioned head buster who doesn't know he's living in the twentieth century. He doesn't know his asshole from a hole in the ground. He's hardheaded dumb, he's stupid enough to make me puke, and he's holding up progress in that local. His unit happened to be the one we needed for an experiment, and he wouldn't cooperate."

"Hold it. An experiment? What the hell do you mean, Jerele? You know the headquarters has veto rights on everything you want to do. We didn't find a single request from you."

"Tough shit. Hold your temper and I'll tell you about it. We're setting up an experiment for a mas-

29

sive shutdown on a limited-time basis of the entire communications network in the States. The whole country will be paralyzed. We shut off the spigot for two-to-four hours, not enough to hurt anything, but enough to give the brass at the big communications companies something to think about. We'll have them crawling. We can ask for almost anything and they'll jump to give it to us. Hell, they'll write a new contract for every union they got and spread on the honey."

"And you've got a test set up to do that?"

"Damned right. Power, that's the only thing those bastards understand. Power, union power, labor power. And then we stick it to them good. But this is just a goddamned test, and your man told us to ram it up our noses in Hollywood. So we sent over a man to talk some sense into his head. He decided to take a short vacation so his union men couldn't blame him. I heard he was taking his secretary and flying to Hawaii for a week.

"Evidently a common courtesy. We have executive loan service for some of the smaller locals. We use them to help out unions in every aspect of the communications industry labor movement."

"Damned generous of you, Jerele."

"We think so. It's good for our image."

"The problem is Butler's wife has reported him missing now, and his secretary has also reported him missing. The cops have found smears of blood on Mr. Butler's office floor. Yesterday they dug a .22 caliber slug out of the wall behind Butler's desk."

"Hell, Butler is your man, not mine. I don't keep tabs on your men. But my guess is that this guy you called Butler probably wanted to get away, so he called my outfit for a standby. We get calls like that all the time."

"Why wouldn't he just let his vice-president take over until he got back, Jerele?"

"How the hell should I know, ask Butler."

"We don't think anyone is going to see Mr. Butler ever again."

"Left for good?"

"We thought maybe you could tell us that, Mr. Jerele, and we don't like it. This is supposed to be a cooperative operation you have here, not some god-damned laboratory for violence. We put up a lot of money to get your group off the ground, and you're supposed to keep us informed of any big plans."

"We know that, Mr. Adams. And I've told George how much we appreciate it a dozen times. It's mutually beneficial. Now if you've got a man with hot pants for some broad he took to Hawaii or to La Paz, that's your problem, not mine. Hell, if you don't want my man there, I'll tell him to pull out."

Adams paused before he replied. "The problem is that local doesn't have a good strong second man."

"So?"

"Hell, we'll leave your man there for now. But if we find out you had anything to do with Butler's bugout, you're going to be in big trouble. George will pull the money rug right out from under your fat little feet."

"Fuck off, Adams!" Victor said and slammed down the phone. His face clouded somewhere between thunder and lightning, then he relaxed and grinned, then he laughed.

Victor turned the rest of the lights off on the board and went from the room. It had no windows; it was his command center, and the assembly of all his security devices were there, as well as some of his more interesting firearms.

He went into the patio, found Mello suntanning topless beside the pool.

"Hey, the men are watching you," he yelled.

"So let them watch. They've seen boobs before. If

not, they can look all they want."

"Dammit, at least get in the water."

She rose, posed on the side, then dove topless into the water.

Victor grinned at her and started pulling off his pants so he could jump in after her.

Chapter 3

ZEROING DOWN TO TARGET

Mark Hardin stared at the status board in the communications room deep in the Stronghold. On it were the ten most critical crime situations in America as the professor categorized them. They used police teletype, newspapers, radio and TV all to chart the important crimes of violence that might qualify for the board. Little slipped by the professor and Mark's watchful eyes. But this time the items on the board held little interest for Mark: a minor revolt by sheepherders in Idaho claiming a new outbreak of dangerous poisonous gas released by the army; a loan-sharking operation flourishing in Miami that led to murder; a sudden rash of prostitutes and call girls flooding Washington, D.C. He scanned the teletype just coming in, tore off a long sheaf of the yellow paper and read it.

A panty hose strangler had struck again in New Jersey; arrests for marijuana had soared again as the screws were tightened, cocaine still being the elite's social drug; and the Russians were using steroids again on their athletes. Then an item caught his interest: Chicago had experienced sabotage in one of its main switching stations and sixty thousand phones were off the hook. Repairs would take up to a week on some circuits. The Chicago PD reported that from all physical evidence at the scene, gasoline and army white phosphorous grenades were used to start the inferno.

Mark took the item to the professor. Willard Haskins sat in a soft chair watching the noon news on TV. Mark gave the retired USC geology professor the item and he read it.

"Another one. I've had a file going on these."

"I hoped that you might. Then there has been more than one problem like this caused by sabotage?"

"Not all of them are sabotage. But that and what looks like a deliberate attempt to cut off some of the communications systems and you've about got it."

Ten minutes later Mark had worked through all the material in the professor's file marked "Communications Trouble." A microwave station had been dynamited, union walkouts had affected several TV operations. There was a related story about a Hollywood union president vanishing, and another man moving into his place temporarily.

Mark thought about the phones out in Chicago. If a large group of landlines went down it could seriously cripple the military. The armed forces used a system called Autovon, Automatic Voice Network that AT&T had worked out for them several years ago. When Mark knew last it involved some 530,000 telephones around the world, all patched together into the military's communication lifeline. The system was set up in such a way that the top brass could break through any busy circuit and get to the party needed.

Top-ranking officers' phones automatically preempted busy circuits in any emergency and their call would go directly through. At one time the military said that a top-priority call could go through in ten seconds to any phone in the military system throughout the world, including SAC bombers in flight, ships at sea, subs, or missile bases.

The ultimate priority rested with the president's red phone, which would clear the line at once to any of the 530,000 drops. Next in the priority line came the Joint Chiefs of Staff's phones.

If someone knocked out a major phone center such as Chicago, Washington, or New York, the Autovon system could be seriously compromised. Mark was aware of the complicated radio network the military employed, but he was also well experienced in how fragile radio communications could be over long distances. Sometimes a two-thousand-mile transmission came through loud and clear, and sometimes sunspots and bad weather caused the signal to break up so badly from a mile away that not a word could be identified. If the Autovon went out, it would be a serious matter for the armed forces, and for the nation's defense.

Mark studied the reports again and picked up the same name in two stories: the National Communications Council of America. He looked up the headquarters, and found it was in Phoenix. Mark got on the police teletype, which was set up so he could send as well as receive. They had tied in the wire with the San Bernardino sheriff's office entirely without the sheriff's knowledge, and it had been working as an excellent adjunct to their information-gathering system for several years.

Mark flipped the machine to SEND and tapped out the message:

35

POLICE BUSINESS****
OPEN MESSAGE
THURGOOD SENDING #114-411pd. AZTEC,
CA. PD
TO: UNIFORM CRIME NETWORK, USDOJ,
ALL LEA
SUBJECT: NATIONAL COMMUNICATIONS
COUNCIL OF AMERICA. GHQ. PHOENIX,
INFORMATIONAL. SEEKING FELONY IN-
VOLVEMENT, CHARGES, CRIMINAL AC-
TIVITY OF THIS UNION OR OFFICERS.
CONFIDENTIAL INVESTIGATION. DO NOT
CONTACT SUSPECT. NEED UNION OF-
FICER NAMES, ACTIVITIES, RECENT AC-
TIONS. URGENT, PHOENIX LEA & AREA
ASKED TO RESPOND.
THURGOOD, AZTEC, CA. PD SENDS.
EOM

Mark watched the teletype spit out the words as
he typed them, then it went back to squirting out
messages from all over the country concerned with
police business.

The wire shifted to a local mode and most of the
material came from California and Arizona. He
watched it awhile, but saw no response from Phoenix and went back to his files. There had to be a
hint somewhere if the Communications Council were
behind any of this union hooliganism. Was it a
concentrated action or only chance that unhappy
employees in three locations resorted to dynamite to
make their feelings known to the company?

Returning to the teletype Mark pulled the long
scroll of continuous printout from the telex machine
and looped it over the desk as he scanned it. Halfway down he found a response from Phoenix:

POLICE BUSINESS****
OPEN MESSAGE
FROM: PHOENIX PD #122–412 PD WIL-
BUR
TO: THURGOOD, AZTEC, CA. PD
RE: NATIONAL COMMUNICATIONS
COUNCIL OF AMERICA
SUBJECT INVOLVED THIS AGENCY TWICE
LAST TWO YEARS. ONE CASE RULED
ACCIDENTAL DEATH FROM FALL
DOWNSTAIRS. QUESTIONABLE CIRCUM-
STANCES, BUT NO WITNESSES, NO MO-
TIVE, NO PROSECUTION. SECOND CASE:
DISCHARGING FIREARM WITHIN CITY
LIMITS. MISDEMEANOR, PAID $25 BAIL
FINE. INVOLVED: VICTOR JERELE, 38,
WHITE MALE. NO PRIOR ARRESTS OR
CONVICTIONS THIS JURISDICTION. RESI-
DENT PHOENIX FOR LAST 3 YEARS: 1414
SUNDESERT ROAD. WILBUR, PHOENIX,
PD SENDS. EOM

Mark considered it. Possible. Just possible that
there was some connection. It wouldn't take long to
run over to Phoenix and find out. Yes, Mark decided, he would fly over that afternoon.

As he was getting ready to go, another response
came on the teletype. It was from the FBI. He read
the message quickly. The bureau had nothing on the
National Communications Council, but they did
have three inquires about it in the last week. It had
been on the watch list because of the potential of
large-scale strike action that would mean serious
hazards to national defense. The data was signed by
Goodman, FBI, Washington. Mark chuckled. That
must be the same Howard Goodman. He'd be furious if he knew that he had actually helped the Pene-

trator. For over five years Goodman had a special assignment by the FBI to capture the Penetrator, and he had failed. Now, evidently, he had been reassigned to the Washington office.

Mark arrived in Phoenix late that afternoon, rented a car at the airport and checked into a Holiday Inn. He left the air-conditioned room and went for a daylight drive past 1414 Sundesert Road. It was in an exclusive enclave near Scottsdale. A high desert-sand-colored slump brick wall in front masked most of the house from the street, but Mark could see that it was two stories and expensive. The driveway had an electrically controlled, black wrought iron gate that rolled back on demand on a pair of twelve-inch rubber-mounted wheels.

Mark drove back to his hotel and got Jerele's number from information, then dialed.

"Yes, Communications Council," a male voice answered.

"Is Mr. Jerele there?"

"Who is calling, please?"

"I'm Randy Scott with the *National Enquirer* newspaper."

"Just a moment."

When the next voice came on the line Mark tried to picture the man but couldn't. The inflection, the tone, nothing gave away any physical characteristics.

"Yes, I'm Victor Jerele. What can I do for you. Always glad to help out the press."

"Thank you, Mr. Jerele. Some union people aren't always so cooperative. You've probably heard of the recent problem with the phones in Chicago. The sabotage that knocked out sixty thousand for almost a week. You were mentioned in an article on the news wires as deploring such criminal action on the part of some vindictive worker. My editor wondered if your group has any plans to shut down any

38

major segment of the country's communications system in protest. It's obvious you have that power now that you have organized the firms that you would need. Is this type of tactic one that your council will pursue as a bargaining ploy in the future? The national contract for communications workers comes up next August I believe."

Jerele laughed. "Well, Mr. Scott, that's a whole group of questions." He was feeling expansive and hoping for some good national exposure in the widely distributed tabloid. "I can only say that any union is going to utilize its strike power to the ultimate if it is pushed by the employers. Just what our ultimate power is, I'm not going to say, Mr. Scott. But as president of this group of unions, I would be failing in my job, in my trust by the members, if I did not do everything proper and legal to gain new and basic human rights benefits for my workers. Were you aware that some communications workers who are not organized are working for twenty cents below the national minimum wage? Now that is a travesty of justice by management."

"Then what you're saying is that your union group does have the power to shut down the telephone company in every aspect of its operation all across the nation, if you want to."

Jerele laughed. "Now, Mr. Scott. You know better than that. We have fragmented contracts, we don't have a national contract with the fifty or sixty Bell Telephone companies. If we did it would be much simpler, wouldn't it?"

"Then do you have plans to utilize other methods for some type of massive shutdown of the nation's communications?"

"I don't see why you ask that, Mr. Scott."

"Well, that must be the basic reason for a large, strong union trust such as you have. It's a conglomerate of communications unions. Why else gather them, unless you want to use them in massive and powerful action against the companies to gain better worker conditions and pay scales?"

"Who are you, again?"

"Randy Scott, from the *National Enquirer*."

"You seem to know a lot about labor relations."

"I'm the labor reporter, here, Mr. Jerele. I've been covering and evaluating labor news for the past fifteen years. I've also followed the creation of your own union group during the past three years."

"Well, I'm flattered, Scott. But I'm afraid you won't find any big front-page exposé on our group. We're only hardworking union stiffs trying to get another 7½ cents an hour for our people."

"The old song was 7½ cents, Mr. Jerele, but now I'm sure you're shooting for 7½ percent instead. Well, thanks for the talk. I'll get back to you later if I have any more questions. Oh, is it true that you now have eleven different national communications workers unions under your umbrella?"

"Eleven? God, I wish we did. Actually we have seven and a few scattered independent locals."

"Right, and thanks, Mr. Jerele, I'll stay in touch."

Mark put down the phone and studied it, but the black plastic handset told him nothing. He would need a soft recon. If he found nothing he would go back to the Stronghold and see what developed. But he had a hunch, he had a feeling, and his hunches in these cases were seldom wrong.

The man had been too slick, too sleek. He had known all the right answers; he even anticipated some of the questions.

Mark slid into his black turtleneck shirt and his black pants, much like those used by stagehands working theater in the round. He left the shirt outside his pants so he could conceal Ava, his dart gun, under it on one side and his .45 on the other. Then

40

he settled down for a nap, with his automatic mental alarm set to go off precisely at 2:00 A.M.

At 2:30 that morning, Mark was parked half a block from the Sundesert Road address. This would be a soft recon, so he would not be seen or noticed, or make contact with any of Jerele's people. He was looking for information that would tie in Jerele with any of the recent violence in the communications industry. Mark had a strong suspicion, but that wasn't enough.

From his daylight drive-by Mark had spotted certain elements that made him guess the house and grounds were both tightly guarded and protected. This was not just another suburban house and garage. He had seen floodlights in the palm trees, and the alarm wire strung along the top of the block fence.

If he guessed right from the outward signs he could see, the place was a fortress. Mark eased out of the car and walked toward the house. It backed against an even more imposing residence and fence on the next block so there was no chance of getting in that way.

Mark leaned against a palm tree and surveyed the block. No one moved, not a dog barked and there was no traffic. He darted toward the wall and angled along it on a soft carpet of the next door neighbor's grass. Under the shadow of a tree, Mark climbed the block fence easily, stepped over the two trip-wires on top, and stared hard into the yard on the other side.

There would be impact sensors there, perhaps even audio sensors. The crooks as well as the good guys were now using the latest in sensing equipment. Mark walked down the top of the fence for ten feet, avoiding the wires. There he came to a short, strange-looking tree which he used to swing softly down to the ground.

Mark paused, his *sho-tu-ca* night vision now allowing him to see the yard of the Jerele house as if it were predusk. The ancient Cheyenne Indian dog soldier's medicine had been taught to Mark by David Red Eagle at the Stronghold. Red Eagle was a Cheyenne medicine chief and still followed many of the old ways. Mark was half Cheyenne himself and had accepted the training years ago. Hundreds of times the knowledge had proved valuable to him.

He smelled the dog before he saw it. He had out Ava, his silent CO-2 powered dart gun. The big German shepherd came out of the darkness without a growl or a sound. Mark had turned and raised the dart gun and the first missile from Ava caught the big dog in the throat as he leaped for Mark. The Penetrator moved at the last instant and the dog flashed past him, crumpled on the grass and twitched for a few seconds before the sodium Pentothal and M-99 tranquilizers put him to sleep.

The dog was big, one hundred twenty-five pounds at least, so the knockout dose designed for a one-hundred-sixty-pound man would not harm the animal, just keep it unconscious for a longer time.

The dart gun, the darts, and the tranquilizers had been developed by Mark and the professor at the Stronghold. Included in the dose was a special muscle spasming agent. Instantaneously on contact with the bloodstream or nervous system, the agent caused dozens of voluntary muscles to go into sudden and painful spasms. This kept a gunman from turning and shooting everyone in sight before the tranquilizers took their ten seconds to render him unconscious.

Mark listened. His sensitive hearing could make out only the shallow breathing of the dog. Nothing else came to him. There could still be a human guard. He worked around the side of the house to the backyard, skirted the pool, then tried the patio

42

sliding glass door but it was locked. Mark saw an open window on the second floor and went up the side of the stucco building silently, using the plentiful finger and toeholds like a human fly, got to the window easily, and stepped inside.

A nude girl lay on the bed. The air conditioning had been turned off. She was on her back, one arm thrown over her forehead, the other spread to one side on top of the satin sheet.

Mark moved like a soft breeze across the room, slipped out the door into a hall, and listened. He could hear persons breathing in each of the next two rooms, but the last one on the end was silent. He opened the door and looked inside. It was a room without windows. Mark didn't need to turn on the lights. He saw a large display board over six feet long with a map of the States on it and main cities shown as well as electrical lines running to light bulbs all over the map. He saw a key on the bottom. It was a map showing the major lines of communications for the different media across the country. Mark found a clipboard on a table that had a code on it, showing names opposite numbers. He took the page off and folded it and put it in his pocket. A national union could have such a display board. It probably meant nothing.

Mark moved to the next room, found nothing of value and was about to go down the stairs to the first floor when he saw a man coming up the stairs toward him.

There was no way to avoid the man or hide. Mark darted him with an Ava sleep dart. It slanted through his T-shirt and injected the solution into the guard's chest. Before the man saw Mark or knew what happened he was twitching and groaning; his legs buckled, and he slid softly down the first few steps like a broken rag doll. By the time he came to a stop at the bottom, he was unconscious. Mark judged his size and decided the man would not be out more than fifteen minutes.

A quick search of the downstairs showed only living and housekeeping rooms, no offices, no boardroom, no meeting room. Toward the back of the house Mark found one windowless room, but he couldn't locate a door into it. That puzzled Mark, but it was past time he was moving.

He walked to the front door, opened it, locked it again with the inside handle, then stepped out and closed the door. He walked openly down the sidewalk and along it to his car.

It wasn't right. It bothered him and he didn't know why. Jerele had too much protection for the home of a union boss. He must have something to hide at that location, but Mark couldn't figure out what it was.

As Mark drove away, a small, quiet motorcycle without lights pulled out and followed him. The man on the cycle grinned, monitoring an audio beeper in his earphone. He got a steady pinging from the bug he had planted on the car bumper of the stranger's rented car just after he went over the wall. The cyclist would follow the stranger back to his house, then find out for sure who he was and whom he worked with before he killed him. It never was enough to lop off the head of one rattler. You had to follow the first back to its nest of snakes so you could get them all at the same time.

Chapter 4

LENNY FREAKS FAR OUT

Mark drove along Indian School Road on the way back from the Scottsdale area with a feeling of tension, as if the night's work wasn't over yet. Something was wrong. He watched the rearview mirror for two miles. Nobody was tailing him. He had slowed and speeded up and saw no pair of headlights keeping up with him, most honked angrily and stormed around him.

Still he had a feeling of being followed. Mark reestablished his *sho-tu-ca* night sight powers and, when he was ready, looked around and in back. He checked the rearview mirror and stared hard into the reflected light. At a stoplight he made the study again and this time he caught something new. Almost a block behind him he saw a motorcycle with the lights off rolling along slowly toward him. The man was out of the light traffic and watching behind him for cars. Why would he be tempting fate with his lights off in traffic?

Mark made a turn down an intersecting street and came to another light, slowing so he would hit the red. He watched again the rearview and saw the same man on the unlighted bike. He wore a gold and silver helmet. Mark had a tail after all.

The Penetrator drove to Seventh Street and turned left, heading back to the center of town. He remembered a parklike avenue that was being expanded; lots of houses and small businesses had been torn down, and the area looked as though it was waiting for the landscaper's crew. He turned into the area suddenly, speeded up, and went around three corners before he stopped quickly at the curb and darted behind a large palm tree before the motorcycle was in sight.

It was only a minute before the soft purr of the well-muffled cycle sounded down the street. The rider passed Mark's car without apparently looking at it, turned at the far corner, and came back. This time he stopped at the driver's side window and checked the interior. He sat there on his bike, his hands on his hips.

Mark moved like a gentle wind in the treetops, making no sound whatsoever as he came up behind the man. Mark tapped the rider at the base of his skull with the hard side of his right hand and the man collapsed, unconscious.

The Penetrator dumped the rider in the front seat of the rented Ford and drove back out seventh Street until it turned into Cave Creek Road, and then found a suitably uninhabited section where he could reason with the biker without any undue interference. As Mark pulled past a stub wall of a torn-down building and parked a half block into a deserted field, the biker came back to life.

"What the hell?" he growled. He found his hands bound behind his back and his ankles strapped together with thick plastic riot cuffs. "Hey, what the hell is going on? Who are you?"

"I'm asking the questions. We can do this simply or we can do it with lots of pain and screaming and blood, all yours. How do you want it?"

"Who the hell are you, anyway?"

"I'm the guy you were following from Victor Jerele's house. Now, who are you?"

He was nervous, mad, but not beaten, Mark watched him trying to figure it out. He was nearly six feet tall, slender with red hair under the helmet, pale brown eyes, and a long nose. Mark guessed he was about twenty-five. He had carried a .32 automatic before Mark took it. The billfold showed only a driver's license, draft card, and Master Charge credit card, the basic ID for almost anyone.

"Lenny, is that what Jerele calls you? Len, maybe. Look, Lenny, it's getting late and I haven't got a lot of time to fool around. I could start by cutting off your finger, but experience has shown me that cutting up people is a bad way to get their cooperation. I always get excited watching the blood ooze out, and then I get carried away, and first thing you know my subject winds up bleeding to death. No sense in that. We both lose."

Mark lifted his right leg and unwound a strip of heavy material from it. It had been fastened with velcro. It had a series of small pockets in it with snaps. Six vials of fluid rested there in sterile ampules. The large pocket held a 3cc syringe.

The display from Mark's leg held Lenny's total attention.

"What do you want, Len, potluck? Why not just pick a color and I'll shoot you up and you can wait and find out what happens. I have all sorts of joy-juice here; you'll have a ball. Oh, careful of the red one there. You like that color? That's curare, a highly deadly poison—you'd be dead in ten seconds,

47

after it hit your system. I know, the white one. That's an especially virulent strain of smallpox. You'd get the best of care and you might even pull through, but that face of yours would probably be so pitted . . . Now, Lenny, who are you and what are you following me for?"

"You know who I am, Lenny Slawson. I'm outside security at the house. You figured that out too. So I must work for Jerele. That's all I know."

"Fine, Lenny. Fine. You won't mind if I just double-check?"

Mark had slid one of the vials from the pouch, filled the syringe with the greenish-tinged fluid and efficiently jabbed the needle into Lenny's upper arm. He pushed the plunger and the fluid injected before Lenny could do more then yelp.

"That wasn't so bad now, was it?"

"What was that stuff?"

"Nothing to worry about. You'll be up and around in just a few weeks. You're liable to get a little sleepy, Lenny, but that's fine, just relax and go with it. Eyes getting a little droopy?"

Mark leaned back in the seat and let himself relax. He had about five minutes before the sodium Pentothal would put Lenny in the right state for questioning. He wouldn't be unconscious or sleeping, but somewhere in between and would answer any question with total honesty. It was slow, and had to be done carefully, but in this case time was no big factor. Mark needed to know everything he possibly could about Jerele and his operation. The fact that there was an outside motorcycle security man now heightened Mark's suspicions.

Fifteen minutes later, Mark was nearly done with the questions.

"You say Sunday a big event will take place?"

"Yes."

"August tenth, is that right?"

48

"Yes, August tenth."

"What event is it?"

"Don't know. Didn't tell me."

"Something is happening Sunday?"

"Yes."

"Where, Lenny?"

"Don't know. Didn't tell me."

"Does Victor Jerele know?"

"Yes, but didn't tell me."

Mark sat back in the car seat and turned off the overhead light. He had all the man knew. He had come at it from four different directions and the answers were all the same; Lenny simply didn't know what Jerele was planning. The obvious kept hammering at Mark. Why else set up a nationwide group of communications unions if you weren't going to shut off the whole damned thing, block out all communications in the nation. But why on Sunday? So it would have less effect on the country? That wouldn't be what the union would want. They would strive for maximum effect, hit as hard as possible. Then why Sunday? Somehow it just didn't match up.

Lenny was a small cog in the Jerele operation, and they simply didn't tell him everything. Only one or two of them perhaps knew. Whatever it was he had a timetable now . . . Sunday, the historical time for a sneak attack on America, such as Pearl Harbor back in 1941. What was the bombshell that was going to hit this time, this Sunday?

Mark got out and went around to the passenger's side. He used his knife to cut the plastic riot cuffs from Lenny's ankles and saw that the effect of the drug was wearing off. He helped him out of the car and sat him on the grass. Mark left the wrists cuffs on. He slapped Lenny gently and the man looked up, his eyes still fogged.

"Lenny, you're going to be all right, you just

relax and sleep a while. When you wake up you'll be your old nasty self again. You may have a little walk to find your bike, but it's probably still there. If you tell your boss how I took you so easily, he'll probably fire you, so why not just forget all about it."

Mark got in the car and drove away, leaving a confused Lenny staring after him.

What next? This was Thursday, August seventh. He had two more full days and whatever was left on Sunday. What should he do, blast into Jerele's fortress and try to blow up the headquarters? Would that stop the operation? It probably wasn't even happening here in Phoenix. If it were a communications blackout, it would be nationwide. Could he possibly find Jerele and make him talk? Jerele might not have told anyone but his top lieutenant what was happening.

Mark remembered the piece of paper he'd taken off the clipboard. He pulled over on the road, stopped, and turned on the overhead light. The paper meant little. It had a series of numbers and areas and communications facilities. Then he saw the checks. One was beside Chicago and sixty thousand phones. One was next to another number that was listed as "microwave tower, Rockies." A third was in Los Angeles and labeled Local 452. The other one was for another microwave tower in Atlanta.

The four points that had been shut off or made ready to shut off yesterday, the sixth. A test. He had been running a test. Sunday he would shut off all seventy-five points on the big board in his map room. But why? Mark drove again. It was almost 4:00 A.M. by the time he got to his motel. Inside he sat on the bed and thought about it.

He could fly to Los Angeles, talk to the two union people he wanted to interview there, and then double-check with Dan Griggs at the Justice Department to see if he had heard anything about a communications blackout set for Sunday.

He had to go to Los Angeles. He could check out and be at the airport for the early-bird six-thirty flight for the City of Angels. He should be there by nine, have all day for the talks and even get back to Phoenix on the evening flight if he needed to.

Mark made his plans after turning in the rental car, and slept all the way to Los Angeles. By 9:30 A.M. he was standing outside of the second floor offices of the Communications Workers of America Local 452. He went in and found himself smiling at a plain girl with last year's style clothes and a hairdo straight out of the 1940s.

"Good morning, may I help you?" she asked, her voice like a soft bell.

"Yes, I'm Randy Scott with the *National Enquirer*. I talked with Mr. Victor Jerele yesterday in Phoenix and he suggested that I stop by here and talk with your new union executive. Is he in?"

"Oh, yes, sir. His name is Doug Slattery. Just a moment and I'll tell him you're here."

Mark looked at the union pictures on the wall. He heard her talking to someone on the phone and turned when she called.

"Mr. Slattery can see you now. Right in this way." She held the door for him and he walked into the room where he figured that the local's president had been cut down so a new team player could take over, at least for a few days.

Slattery rose and held out his hand. He was smaller than Mark had expected, about five eleven, and overweight. "Well, the press. We usually don't get this kind of attention. What seems to be the big story you're working on?"

"I had hopes that you might tell *me* that, Mr. Slattery."

51

Slattery was all smiles but underneath Mark felt the man tense and go on the defensive.

"I'm sorry, but I lost you. What are you here for? What can I tell you about Local 452?"

"The local's president vanished. Your assignment is to fill in and handle normal business until he comes back or the local members take some action. It's always interesting to me as a labor writer when a labor leader vanishes suddenly with no explanations and no trace. We call it the Jimmy Hoffa syndrome. Some people call it the lead overcoat or the Jimmy Hoffa cement boots."

Slattery's face stiffened just a little but the smile was still there, cold and formal. "Oh, I see. You're digging, trying to build something out of nothing. Marvin Butler went on vacation, didn't they tell you that?"

"Strange that he wouldn't even tell his wife or his secretary, don't you think?"

He kept smiling, but got up and walked around the office. "You've never been a labor leader, Mr. Scott, I can tell that. The pressures are tremendous. Not just from the members, from all sides: management, national leaders, the press, civic officials. It all builds and builds and builds until some men have to get away, to take a break. Now I don't know Marvin Butler, but I've heard he is a good, conscientious union man, fine family man and father. That's the kind of guy this all hits at the hardest. In a week I predict Marve will come back, swinging in here with a tan, and an extra five pounds and eyes just a little bloodshot and be raring to go."

"Mr. Slattery, you're from the National Communications Council's executive loan pool, is that right?"

"Yes, I fill in on jobs like this from time to time when we are asked."

"And you know Victor Jerele?"

"Of course. He's our president and executive director."

"In Phoenix?"

"That's right, Mr. Scott."

Mark took a gamble. If the hit were made there in the office, the chances are there was some blood around. The police are experts at finding traces of quickly wiped up blood.

"Mr. Slattery, did you know that the police found blood smears on the floor of this office? I'm not sure where it was, the cops wouldn't say, but it was human blood and recently spilled."

Mark watched Slattery's smile change into a passive, cold stare. He stood. His eyes turned furious and he pointed to the door.

"Out!"

"How does it feel, Slattery, to be a stand-in for a murdered man? Give you a cold tingle up your spine? Ever wonder when your number might be up and Jerele decides you know too much?"

Slattery started to move from his desk, but when Mark stood and looked down at him, he stopped.

"Get out, now, or I'll call the police."

Mark laughed. "Now that would be a switch, you calling the police for protection. A real belly slapper." Mark sobered. "Look, Slattery, I don't like people like you, and I'm going to get you and your phony union. You can tell Jerele that. I think Butler was killed by you or your people right here in this office and his body deep-sixed out in the Pacific Ocean somewhere. Now he's nothing but shark bait. You can tell Jerele that too." Mark turned and left the office and saw the shaken man reaching for the telephone.

The Penetrator nodded to the secretary, then continued out the door, into the hall, and to the stairs at the end of the corridor. He was taking his time, hoping that Slattery would make some play against

53

him. He almost needed it as a sign that he was on the right scent.

It took longer than Mark expected. He left the building, looked at the address, wrote it down in his pocket note pad, and was almost to his car before a medium-sized man hurried toward him.

"Mr. Scott?" the man called while still twenty feet away.

Mark was about to go around to the driver's side of the car, but he paused and tensed. No one else could know that name but someone from Slattery's office.

"You forgot something in the office . . ."

The man carried a small book in his hand. He held it out to Mark, and when he was close enough drove his other hand forward in a stiff-fingered jab at Mark's solar plexis. Mark spun away, chopped down with his right hand in a vicious swing, and at the same time blocked a kick from the other man.

Mark faced his attacker again, taking the "triangle" stance ready for an attack from any angle. But the attacker had spun away and run a few steps holding his left wrist as he walked quickly down the block. He looked over his shoulder once, and Mark saw the agonizing pain on the face; but the man hadn't even cried out. Mark guessed he had a broken wrist; it should have been from the force of his blow. It would be a day to remember for the attacker, and a lesson learned: never underestimate your opponent.

Mark watched the man out of sight, got in his car and drove. As he passed the office building he looked up and saw Slattery standing in the window, watching his car.

Back at his in-town headquarters, a small restaurant on Wilshire where he knew the manager, Mark made a call to the Stronghold. He reported his actions so far and suspicions. The professor had some new information.

"In Orange County, right there near Los Angeles, there's been another communications union disciplined. The vice-president is in the hospital and he's talking to everyone who'll listen. He also has a police guard, twenty-four hours, and a date with the grand jury as soon as he can move."

"I'll go talk to him," Mark said. He told the professor about the "big event" coming up Sunday and asked him to make some probes about what it could mean, check the future calendar, and see how it could affect communications. Mark got the union man's name and hospital and signed off. After a quick lunch he drove to the Bedford Hospital in Orange. Mark had his fake Justice Department ID, so there shouldn't be any problem with his weapons. One cop doesn't pat down another one.

At the hospital Mark found the right room and showed his Justice Department ID to the cop sitting outside the door. He was properly impressed, but went inside with Mark, locked the door, and leaned against the wall.

"Orders," he said. "Anytime he's got visitors, I got to be inside and the door locked."

"Right," Mark said.

José Rodriguez lay in bed with one leg in traction suspended a foot from the bed. His head was bandaged so only his eyes and mouth showed, and one hand was in a cast protecting a broken thumb.

"Hey, man, *qué pasa?*"

Mark grinned. Nothing much was happening for José. "Amigo, looks like some jealous husband caught you in the wrong bed."

José laughed. "I wish he had. One on one I don't mind, not me. I'm a talker, you heard. I talk to everybody the cop lets in. But I don't talk to no more goddamned union brass. You, I'll talk to. You want

55

to know why I caught this? I get a phone call, says pull out our men, nobody to work on Sunday, August tenth. I say we got a contract, a good one; no way I can pull my men. They say tough shit, pull out the men. But if we break the contract, we lose it, and they don't care, pull off men Sunday. I tell them to go take a hike, throw this little guy right out of my office. Next day two big gringos come in and work over me and my office."

José looked out the window. A tear slid down from one brown eye. "They hurt me bad. One two-hundred-pounder jumped on my leg. The other one held me down and he jumped and broke my knee somehow. Doctors say it's a miracle I'll be able to walk again. Now I do everything I can to get back at those goons. I looked through a thousand mug shots from the police, but they ain't local. Neither one said a word, man, they just crash in and bust me up. I get one with my knife, man, but don't cut him bad. He take the cut on the arm so he can get my blade away and my fight is all over. They just bashed me around after that."

"All because of Sunday. Something big is going down Sunday, José, do you know what it is? Did they say anything?"

"Not a word."

"Think back to your union meetings, your talk with them on the phone. Is there anything that might hint at the tenth of August?"

José shut his eyes, rubbed his bandaged head gently with his unmarked left hand.

"No, amigo, nothing I remember."

"Have you ever heard of the National Communications Council of America?"

"No." He paused. "Yeah, that was the name of the outfit the guy on the phone was from. He said our union was a member of it and in a solidarity move we had to walk out Sunday."

"The guys who worked you over must have been from that outfit then, wouldn't you say?"

"Yeah, I remember now. That's what I told the cops. That's what I say on TV last night when they did the story. Today I got so many mad phone calls I had them take out the phone."

"You hear about Local 452?"

"Oh, yeah, a little. Somebody missing I hear."

"I'm not sure, José, but I think they also talked with this guy about some special strike action. You're lucky, José. I'm sure they killed this other dude and fed him to the sharks."

"You bring good news, man," José said; and Mark could hear the bitter humor in his voice.

Mark reached out and shook José's good left hand.

"Hang in there, José; I'm going to get these bastards for you. And that's a promise."

"Thanks, amigo."

The guard followed Mark out the door, had him sign out and put down the time; then Mark went down the corridor to the elevator.

He found a motel near the L.A. International Airport. There was nothing more he could do here. He'd get a good night's sleep to make up some for last night when he was up till dawn. Then he'd be ready to grab an early flight to Phoenix. Western still had one, he thought. He was starting to get fuzzy. Once he let down after a forty-eight-hour day he went weird in a rush.

Mark concentrated then, drove into the parking lot of the motel and got into the room. He didn't even bother to have any food, just locked the door, put on the chain, checked the windows, and went to sleep. He had a feeling he would have a big day the next day.

Chapter 5

ROOM OF NO RETURN

At nine-thirty the next morning Mark sat in his rented Ford in Phoenix looking up the street at the fortress owned by Victor Jerele. He was going in, but he wasn't sure exactly how. He wasn't interested in making a hard hit on the place, not yet. First he had to find out what was happening Sunday and why.

He could try to get in as a Justice Department agent, but they would stop him at the gate and ask for a warrant. A salesman? Real estate? No good. Wind Walker? Might be. The sudden darting movements of the Wind Walker meant he could move right past someone in full view, and the person would have only a sensation of seeing something, but he could not identify the apparition as a person. Mark had been working through the rituals to activate his *sho-tu-ca* powers, the deep thought, the introspection, the ritual words and thoughts to cleanse his mind and spirit.

Mark decided he would try the crazy inventor bit, with a breakthrough in the world of communications that he wanted to give to a union so the workers could get the benefits of it, and not the big corporations. He had no idea what kind of a story he would tell, but now he started the car, drove forward, and stopped in front of the Jerele house. He carried his complete assortment of personal weapons and special devices just in case. Mark was going into a combat situation so he was ready. The Penetrator took a small briefcase filled with worthless papers and stepped from the car.

At once he was aware he was under observation. Some kind of a video camera caught him. He felt it as he walked to the gate and pressed the bell. A speaker came on at once.

"Yes, what do you want?"

"My name is Arthur Handy. I have a supersecret communications breakthrough that I want to give to some union, and I figured yours was the best one. I want the union and the union members to profit from this amazing discovery and not the capitalistic downtrodders."

"Yeah, right, now move along. We ain't got no time for that kind of . . . what? Just a minute." The sound stopped. A moment later another voice came on. It wasn't Jerele; Mark would recognize that voice from the telephone.

"Mr. Handy, good morning. I'd be delighted to see your invention. I'll send a man out to bring you in. You realize we must have certain security measures."

"Oh, right, yes sir. I understand that."

A lock clicked somewhere and a small section of the large wrought iron gate swung open. It was spring-loaded. A man in a sport shirt and slacks came out. He motioned Mark inside, then closed the gate, and Mark heard the lock click.

"Up here," the man said. He was medium height, medium build, medium battle-scarred around the face, and Mark decided medium dumb as well. The man led him around the side of the house to the pool area where Mark had been before. A man sat at a twin-seat redwood lounger that had a small table built between the seats.

The man Mark was to see was small and wiry, balding, with half glasses that swung on a silver chain around his neck. He had a firm handshake.

"Well, Mr. Handy. Sit down, sit down. I used to know a man in Detroit named Handy, Jamison Handy, are you related to him?"

"No, I'm afraid not."

"Oh. Now what is this about an invention that would revolutionize the communications business?"

"Actually it's not really new; it's a different and dramatic application of known technology to the field of personal communications. By juxtapositioning some components in the linear alignment of the basic circuity on the input side of a transceiver, we can rectify and modify the signal so it gives a binary output in the ultralow megahertz range that is so much better than anything now on the market to make it absolutely mind-boggling."

"I'm sure. Could you translate that into English," the small man said.

"I have a detailed rundown in my briefcase—may I?"

The man nodded. Mark realized he was getting nowhere; his bluff was almost over. The muscle was only ten feet away, standing, waiting. There was nothing convincing in his briefcase except Ava. He decided it was time. Mark opened the case so the top was toward both the small man in the chair and the thug. The Penetrator came up with Ava and put one sleep dart into the enforcer before he even saw the gun. Mark dropped the briefcase lid and turned

61

the gun at the small man, who yelped once, then caught a round point-blank in his upper arm. His shirt prevented the dart body from penetrating the skin, but the load of sodium Pentothal in knockout strength and the M-99 and muscle spasming agent were injected and did their work. The small man shook in pain and frustration for ten seconds, then passed out.

Mark closed the briefcase and walked toward a sliding glass door leading inside.

Someone came out as he started in. Mark nodded and vanished inside. The man in the pool area called softly to someone, then he yelled, and Mark ducked behind a big chair just as two more men ran through the room and out the open glass door.

Three live goons so far and two sleepers. Mark ran toward the room he hadn't been able to find a doorway to the night before. That could be the key. For just a second he saw a face peer around a hallway corner at him, then it vanished. The face belonged to Lenny, the biker snitch. Had he recognized Mark? The Penetrator couldn't wait to find out. He ran toward the secret room and again searched for a door along the hall. There was none.

He looked behind and saw a man lifting a gun. Mark fired Ava twice and saw one of the darts hit the man; he went down at once before he could fire. A round came from the other direction, the sound of the .38 weapon ahead booming in the confines of the narrow hallway. Mark lunged to one side then saw a door open just ahead of him. It had seemed to come out of nowhere. He dove toward it and jolted inside before any more shots came. Almost at once something whispered behind him and before he could turn or move the sliding panel slammed shut.

Mark Hardin stood there in total darkness. Seldom had he been in such a lighttight room. There was an absolute lack of light. Even his *sho-tu-ca*

62

sight could not function here, since it only amplified available light. Here there was nothing to concentrate.

He heard something, a click, the tiniest relay closing, and then a guffaw, a chuckle, that boomed into a totally hysterical screaming laugh. The sound trailed off.

"Welcome, Mr. Handy, or whoever you really are. We've been expecting you. Lenny told me about you and your little needles. You play rough. We're not sure just how much he told you, but that's all academic, isn't it? A moot point as the lawyers would say because it really will have no bearing on the outcome of the case. Your case, Mr. Handy, or Mr. Scott, or whoever you are."

"Oh, is it dark in there? Sorry, let me turn on some light."

Mark guessed from the brilliance of the lights that poured into the room that they must be stream lights, the same kind the police use, which have a range of two miles. Now their blinding brilliance was confined in a small area. Before they became too bright for Mark to see anything, he recorded the fact that he was in a kind of a cell within a room, a box, that was no more than an eight-foot cube. The sides seemed to be flawless and smooth. As the brilliance increased Mark closed his eyes and then put his hand over them. His *sho-tu-ca*-ready eyes had been shocked by the high candlepower.

"Oh, you don't like the lights? What a shame. Maybe lights and some of our Arizona heat will make you see things our way. Oh, did I forget to tell you? We'll call off our little light show for you here anytime you want to tell us exactly who you are, who you work for, and why you're here. Incidentally, we know you're not working for the *National Enquirer*. We called Florida and checked with the editor. He had never heard of us, or of you. So that scam is over. Ready to talk now?"

"Jerele, you murdering bastard. I know a lot about you, but I need more. I'm getting a little lynching party together and we want you as the honored guest. We'll spring it on you suddenly, but I think the whole thing will stretch your mind, and then your neck."

The sound came then, and heat was added to the brilliance. Mark tried to cover his ears, but the high-frequency sound exploded all around him and left him numb, his head pounding and throbbing with the intensity of the unbearable sound.

Mark knew he had to think. So many of his skills would not help him in this torture box. The top had been left open; he'd seen that in a flash of the first light. But it was covered with a latticework of bare, reinforcing steel rods—for concrete, probably. They could see inside all the time. He had a limited number of escape devices with him, but he'd have trouble using them if he was being watched all the time.

"The lights! Turn off the lights; they make it too easy for me," Mark bellowed suddenly. A few moments later the lights snapped off.

Mark had stopped as soon as he blundered into the room, and had not moved. The doorway opening had to be somewhere in the wall directly behind him. He spun around and moved back to it, hand in front of him until he touched it. The wall was warm. What did that mean? He felt no electrical charge. His fingers explored the wall critically; yet even his sensitive touch could not find any trace of an opening. He went from one end of the permanent wall to the other, judged the distance to the center, and picked a spot. It didn't matter much if he missed the approximate spot. From his left ankle he unwrapped a quarter-inch-thick sheet of C-4 plastic explosive, about half an ounce. The concussion of the explosion in the small area would be severe, but most of the force would go out the open top of the cell into the large room area and dissipate. Mark decided that he could stand the concussion if he must, and it looked now as though he would need to.

The sound continued, but Mark increased his *sho-tu-ca* mind-block protection, canceling out those nerves that recorded the intense sound waves.

He folded the explosive into a rectangle and plastered it against the wall where he hoped the sliding door might be, and inserted a twenty-second timer detonator pencil designed for easy use in the dark. It was a simple one with a push-pull switch for activation. He didn't set it yet.

Mark slipped from his pocket two tear-gas and nausea balls. They were about the size of a golf ball, and shattered on impact. Mark had used them before. He decided the operators of the cell must be inside the larger room. He could get at them with the nausea gas. Mark had his own handkerchief mask that would filter out most of the gas if it came back inside the cell. He went to the wall opposite the one the door was on and jumped as high as he could next to the wall and felt the top of it. It was about nine feet off the floor. On his next jump Mark pushed one of the gas balls over the edge and heard it fall and shatter outside the cell wall.

Quickly he moved to the adjacent wall and repeated the process and by the time the second ball shattered he heard voices.

"What the hell?"

"What is that stuff?"

"Get your flashlight on."

"Gas! We'll both be killed; let's split!"

Mark heard a door open, and then several feet running. The mike came back on.

"Clever, Mr. Handy, but not nearly enough. I can

operate the cell from well outside the inner room. How would you like to reduce a little?"

As he said it, the wall began to move. Mark touched the outer wall and realized the one with the C-4 was not moving. That had to be the regular house wall. He would use the blast of C-4 at the last possible moment. It was the most dangerous device he had. How far would the wall come in? He felt the end walls, but they weren't moving. Mark held out his arms and soon he could touch both walls. How far?

Quickly he slid a half inch telescoping rod from his right shin, extended it to its full twenty inches, and twisted it, locking the parts together. The short rod had many uses for Mark in the past, as an auxiliary weapon, as an extension for a knife, and the pointed end even worked as a chisel.

Now he held it against the front wall about two feet off the floor and waited as the back came silently toward him. It touched the bar, then pressed forward. The wall stopped moving at the end nearest to Mark, but kept moving at the other end. He heard the first crack, then splintering as the twisted wall couldn't take the strain. He could imagine the cracks in the wall. Suddenly the lights snapped on again and he heard swearing over the speaker, soft, furious, the mutterings of a man near the breaking point.

"You idiot! Nobody has ever damaged my room before! I'll squash you like a bug!"

Mark felt the wall move back. When it was at the farthest point, he ran to the C-4 bomb on the solid wall and pushed and pulled the pencil detonator timer. The one was preset for twenty seconds.

Mark dropped to the floor as far as he could to get away from the explosive. He rolled into a ball, put his hands over his ears as tightly as possible, and left his mouth open. He was in a concentrated ball with only a portion of his back exposed to the brunt of the explosion.

Even before it came he felt the wall moving again; then the next thing he saw a brilliant flash through his eyelids, even though his head was pressed against his knees. The cell shuddered and shook, gravel-sized pieces of the wall ricocheted around the cell like hail and some slammed against him. He didn't think any broke the skin. The pounding, thundering, echoing, booming explosion shook him worse than he thought it would. He rolled on the floor, his ears aching despite his protection. He wouldn't be able to hear for several minutes.

Slowly the dust settled. Mark tried to look around. The brilliant lights were out, probably blown away. Shards of weak light splintered in through a shattered front wall. As he figured, it was the side one where the door was. Mark could sense movement on the other side of the wall away from the light. He sat on the floor, brushed dust and chips of something from his clothes. Then he tried to stand. He made it, and moved slowly toward the light. The lack of sound was eerie, strange. He knew it was his ears, he was temporarily deafened by the blast, but still it was weird. The wall where he placed the charge was torn. Part of it had been blown into the hallway. There was a hole half big enough to crawl through. He kicked with his boots, enlarging it. Then he looked out cautiously each way. It was the hall.

He saw no one. A wild, crazy sound began and he knew it was only in his head, a soft pinging that wouldn't stop. He shook his head and put his hands over his ears, but still it came through like a hard game of Ping-Pong.

Mark kicked his way through the hole and stood in the hall. Still no one was in sight. He ran along the opening back to the living room where he had

67

been first. A television set was on, but there seemed to be no one there. He drew the .45 automatic from his belt as he ran. He had to find Jerele. Now he noticed that the picture window in the living room opening onto the pool area had been cracked by the blast. Everyone must be outside.

For one quaking moment, Mark realized that someone might be shouting at him or even shooting at him and he wouldn't be able to hear. He spun around, watched behind for a moment, then moved into the other rooms on the ground floor. He found no one. Strange. The Penetrator ran to the front room and looked out an unbroken window. A police car had just pulled up at the front gate and two officers got out. They looked at the house, checked in with the squad car radio, and then begin working at the front gate. Mark went out the patio door, saw no one, and in two giant steps, climbed the six-foot wall and jumped over it into the neighbor's backyard. From there he walked to the street and then to his car. The cops had left the front gate, and were at the door of the house.

On the sidewalk in front of Jerele's fence, a smattering of civilians gathered. More people seemed to walk up each minute, attracted by either the explosions or the police cars.

Someone touched his arm and he turned slowly, controlling his first sudden impulse to attack. An elderly man stood there, his lips moving, but Mark heard only a faint murmur. Mark shook his head and pointed to his ears.

"I can't hear you," Mark said. Not even hearing his own words, but he knew he had said them, because the old man nodded and walked on to the excitement. Mark got in his rented car and tried to make his hearing come back. Not even his *sho-tu-ca* powers could put his human ear back into operation. This had happened before with explosions. It was a sudden overload to the inner ear and it seemed to turn itself off for a while to recover. Mark hoped it wouldn't take too long.

He sat there for five minutes and traffic increased. An ambulance came by, and Mark heard the low moan of its siren.

He heard! He looked back to make sure, then listened harder and made out some background sounds. A car whispered past, far off a dog barked, a child shrieked in delight. Now he heard the sound of his own laughing and he grinned.

"This is Mark Hardin coming back on the air after a short technical problem that has now been fixed," he said. The words were soft and whisperish, but he heard them. Soon his ears would be back to normal.

The Penetrator looked at the crowd around the Jerele house. He knew he had to find out who was hurt. If it were Jerele the game might be over. He still had to find the man and convince him to talk. Somehow.

Mark closed the door of his car gently, watched the crowd up the street and then walked that way, casually. He hummed a tune to check on his hearing, and the sound came through stronger. He felt certain enough that he could talk to someone.

There were thirty people on the sidewalk in front of the house now, some hanging over the fence, looking in, others near the ambulance that had backed up to the gate; but no one had been brought out yet. The man-sized gate was open and a policeman stood there keeping away the curious.

Mark blended in with the crowd, and when a man came out on a gurney stretcher, he edged closer to see who it was. He didn't know him. It was not one of the men he had seen before at the house and he hoped it wasn't Jerele.

One of the ambulance men provided the answer.

"No, Mr. Thomas. I don't know where anyone

else is. We got a call to come, so we came. You're the only person we found in the whole place. Now just take it easy, you're not all that bad hurt."

Mark looked around. He saw no one he guessed could be Jerele. He would have to come back later. After the cops had gone, after everyone had left.

The date still pounded at him. Sunday, August tenth. He had to tell someone. Dan Griggs. He got back to his car and drove until he found a telephone booth in a small shopping center away from traffic. Mark placed a collect call from the booth to Dan Griggs in the Justice Department in Washington.

He gave the operator the number from memory and waited.

Dan came on the line feeling frisky.

"Mark? I don't know any Mark. Why the hell should I pay the freight for your long-distance calls?"

"A good afternoon to you, Mr. Griggs. Question: what of importance to the government is happening this Sunday, August tenth?"

Dan's end of the line went silent for a moment, and Mark could imagine Dan scanning his advance calendar. "Mark, not a damn thing that I know about."

"That's the problem—we don't know about it. Something is going to happen, and it won't be good. It has something to do with the communications industry, and the only thing I can come up with is that some attempt will be made to black out the communications network for the entire nation."

"Impossible. Do you know how many lines of communication we have?"

"Yes, and do you know how many of them pass through key microwave relay stations that carry telephone, telegraph, radio, and TV networks?"

"My God, you're right. I saw something about that the other day. Something like eight or ten key

70

relay stations could put down eighty percent of our communications."

"Precisely. I've been sparring with a union called the National Communications Council of America. Ever heard of it?"

"Not so far."

"You will. See what you can dig up on it, and if I were you, I'd have the armed forces crank up some kind of a surprise alert for this weekend, something to keep their radio emergency network alive and working as well as it can. The Autovon is going to be shot all to hell, if this blackout hits the phone system. I've got one more man to see, but thought you should know something about what I've been working on."

"Okay, Mark, you paid for your free call. Anything else happening? I'll get moving on this, but this is Friday. Not a hell of a lot I can do now. I might tell the president, if I can get through that bunch of southerners around him."

"Have fun. If I get anything more definite I'll let you hear."

"Do that. How is the professor?"

"As cranky as you are on a good day. I better get back to work."

They signed off and Mark hung up. He'd known Dan Griggs since his very first campaign. He'd turned out to be a good friend, and he was one of the few persons alive who knew who the Penetrator was and why he was.

Time, that was Mark's biggest enemy now. Time. Friday, 11:00 A.M. A day and a half to Sunday. Jerele still was the key to the puzzle, or at least to the next step.

Mark put coins in the slot and dialed the phone again. He had picked Jerele's number out of his memory banks from the time he called him before.

71

There were eight rings before someone picked up the phone.

"Yeah?"

"Hello, is Sergeant Anderson there?" Mark asked.

"Cops are all gone."

"Good, what about Mr. Jerele?"

"I don't know. He's damned busy."

"Tell him Mr. Scott wants to talk to him."

"Yeah, OK."

When new sound came from the phone it exploded in a rush of words so fast Mark could barely understand them.

"You again? You scheming, goddamned son of a bitch."

"Mr. Jerele, please, I'm easily offended. Are you so angry because your little room broke apart?"

"Yes, and between you and the cops I couldn't get some last-minute work done I needed to, but now I have. Who the hell are you, anyway?"

"Does it matter?"

"Yes. I still want to kill you, to scalp you, to make you die slowly."

"Then come and get me, Jerele."

"Where are you?"

"Listen closely and I'll tell you exactly where I am and how to find me."

"I'm lisening."

Chapter 6

DESERT SUN FOR TWO

Mark had talked to Jerele for five minutes, explaining where he would be and what he was driving, asking Jerele what he drove and making sure the meet could be made. Then Mark gave Jerele a tight deadline and hung up.

Back at the rented Ford, Mark checked the suitcase of weapons in his trunk, took out three thermite grenades, more rounds for Ava, and then picked up the Sidewinder submachine gun and extended the shoulder stock. He took two magazines of the deadly .45 caliber rounds for the weapon and put everything under his coat on the front seat. Then he drove quickly back toward the Jerele house on Sundesert Road. Mark saw activity at the house as he drove by and parked half a block away, turning around so as to have the car headed back toward Jerele's place.

Less than five minutes later Jerele's big blue Cadillac swept out of the drive and turned away from

Mark toward Scottsdale Road. Mark drove up at once, parked across from the house, took the three thermite grenades and walked to the gate. It was locked. He went on past to the same neighbor's lawn he had used before and climbed over the wall. Once inside the wall on Jerele's side he took out Ava and moved to the rear of the house. The sliding glass door was locked.

He broke the lock with a slash of his heel and the aluminum prong fell away, releasing the door. Inside he worked quickly, setting the thermite canisters where they would do the most damage: one in a closet with clothes, another in the hallway next to wood paneling, and a third in the garage under the gas tank of a three-year-old Porsche. Too bad about the car. He activated each canister as he placed it, all with five-minute timers, then went out of the house the way he entered and got back in his car. He doubted that anyone noticed him, and if they did it would be far too late by the time they traced the car. The thermite grenades would go off soon and the furiously burning devices would ignite the house. It would be so far consumed that, by the time the fire department got there, the men would be able to do little except save the houses on each side.

Mark gunned away from the house toward Scottsdale Road. He wasn't sure where he was going, not exactly. He had established a meeting point with a map in hand, and had bluffed beautifully. His purpose was to get Jerele out of town, out of civilization far enough so they could have a friendly chat. He knew Jerle would bring his guns along and all the help he could jam into his Caddy. But that would make it a slightly more even contest.

Mark had set up Carefree as the meeting spot, a small dot of a town on the map thirty miles due north of Scottsdale on Scottsdale Road. Actually it was the end of the road directly north. It was just past the Fort McDowell Indian Reservation and near the Tonto National Forest. Mark had told Jerele he would meet him at the first filling station in the little town. He couldn't miss it. Mark had carefully described the red Porsche 928 he would be driving. Jerele said he'd be in a new Chevy Malibu, a blue one. He had left with his hit men in a blue car, but it was a blue one-year-old Cadillac. At least he knew what Jerele was driving. He grinned and pushed down on the throttle, hoping the Arizona State Police still didn't enforce the double-nickle speed limit.

Mark arrived at the edge of Carefree less than a half hour later and watched for the first filling station. He saw it, Standard, on the right. The blue Cadillac was parked on the side street beside the station, aimed for the highway. Mark drove past, circled to the right on a dusty gravel street a block off the highway, and came up behind the Caddy. Mark knew the men would be watching the station. He paused, then hit the gas and swung toward the Caddy, grazing the side of it in a minor metal-tearing sideswipe; then his car bounced away and he was gone, out on the highway that went through town and headed northeast. Up there were lots of open spaces, the national forest, and the village of Seven Springs, maybe ten miles away.

The Caddy fired up and roared after him, and Mark could see the angry expression on the man's faces. He waved a single middle finger at them and waltzed on through the tiny town, then onto the open highway. The heavily laden Caddy surged ahead trying to catch up. Mark didn't know where he was going, just out of town. Almost anywhere would do.

He stayed on the road for three or four miles, until he was inside the Tonto National Forest; then he took the first good-looking dirt road to the left and plunged into the outback. He was heading into the New River Mountain area, a wilderness with no roads and no people. The map had showed him an area thirty miles long and fifteen miles wide containing mostly the national forest and a lot of not much else.

He had to learn the hard way that a national forest in the Southwest was a far cry from the same thing in Wisconsin or Montana, or Oregon or even northern California. In the high, dry country the forest may consist of a few scrub pine, a mass of mesquite, and some picturesque land more noted for its sagebrush, tall cactus that looked like trees, and smoke trees that looked like a puff of smoke.

He found this forest much like that. Typical outback in Arizona, it was nothing but long stretches of scabby, rolling land, with a few trees, scrub pine and stunted oaks, grass and some mesquite and chaparral once in a while, a few live oaks in the washes, and lots of cactus, rattlesnakes, scorpions, and desert rats.

The road Mark had selected looked like a little-used one. It deteriorated quickly into a twin row of tire tracks with weeds between. There was no way to lose anyone. The tires threw up a cloud of dust that could be seen ten miles away. The Caddy dropped back a quarter of a mile to cut down on the dust and so the driver could see where he was going. The plumes of dust rose a hundred feet in the still, dry air, then slowly began to settle.

Mark kept moving until he found what he wanted. He had driven for about a half hour, and figured he had gone ten miles, not making very good time over the washes and ruts and uneven ground. He stopped at a splash of live oaks in a wash. He turned off the fading track of a road and angled under the nearest tree, a two-foot-thick live oak with branches that reached forty feet into the air. It was the biggest tree he had seen all day. The Penetrator drove the Ford behind the tree, got out, and crouched by the side of the gnarled trunk. There was absolutely no wind.

The temperature in the desert had climbed unseasonably. On the car radio Mark had heard warnings that the lower deserts could expect temperatures from one hundred to one hundred ten degrees. Those were the highest August temperatures all year, and the weatherman were warning the uninitiated about dangers of traveling in the desert.

It had been a weird day all the way around for Mark; no reason the weather should cooperate now. If all went well, he'd find out from Jerele what he needed to know and be back in Phoenix in plenty of time to catch the six-thirty flight for Los Angeles.

The Caddy was having more trouble with the rough road than Mark's Ford, and it came slowly through the dust. When the cloud settled around Mark, he watched the Cadillac stop a quarter of a mile off. They were evidently watching him, perhaps with binoculars.

Mark waited. The Cadillac moved up to within two hundred yards and stopped. It was too far for anything but a rifle shot. Suddenly a bullhorn-amplified voice spat words across the silent desert.

"Mr. Scott, I see you're ready to talk. All right, talk. I have a certain advantage with a mechanical voice. But I assure you I am not going to tell you anything. All I've come out here for is to kill you."

Mark lifted his .45 and estimated the 200-yard range, then sent a shot at the blue car. He grinned as the lucky elevation sent the slug into the blue Caddy's right front fender.

The only answer was a spurt of dust as the car backed up twenty yards. Mark saw the off side door open and two men get out. One ran from rock to rock to Mark's right. The other one made a circling

77

route to the left. Both made sure they stayed far away from Mark. It was the old encirclement, get-behind-them ploy. When the men were almost even with him, one on each side, and some three hundred yards from the Caddy, Mark jumped back in his Ford. He gunned away from the tree and charged head on for the Cadillac. At least half the firepower had left the fort; now was the time to attack.

He had the Sidewinder up and pointed through the driver's window. Mark let loose a burst at fifty yards. Two .45 caliber slugs smashed the windshield and forced the passengers still in the car to the floor. Every three or four seconds after that Mark put two single shots into the Caddy, and then as he came even with it and flashed by at twenty feet, he kept his finger on the Sidewinder until the last of the thirty rounds left in the magazine spewed out and stitched seams along the Caddy's sheet metal.

He took no return fire.

Divide and conquer.

Mark had seen the two soldiers in the encirclement strategy turn and run back toward the Caddy, but they were far too late. He pulled around at a hundred feet and looked back at the target. The blue Cadillac listed to one side where one of the big tires had been punctured, probably by a ricochet.

A back door came open and a man rolled out to the ground. He tried to get up, got to one knee, then slid over backward and didn't move again.

Mark turned the Ford and headed for the nearest of the two field men. This one was a hundred yards from the Cadillac and didn't have a prayer of getting there. Mark cut past the other car at twenty yards and heard one shot, feeling the rear door of the Ford take a slug. The runner saw Mark coming now and got off two shots with a handgun before Mark brought up the Sidewinder. He had put in a new magazine and now sent three rounds at the running man. All missed, but the man heard the machine-gun sound coming at him and he turned into the desert in panic. Mark saw the .45 in the runner's hand as he came up behind him. The man fired again. Mark ducked below the dash but held the steering wheel solidly and kept his foot on the accelerator. The front bumper hit something followed by a scream; then the rear wheels bumped over something else and the car charged on past.

Mark straightened up, trying not to think about the man he had just run down. He turned and stared at the rag-doll lump of humanity behind the car. It wasn't moving. Mark spun the wheel and started for the other man, but he was in the Caddy now and had it moving, back toward the road.

The flat tire flopping on the nonroad made the car creep slowly through the desert. Mark came up behind it and unloaded ten rounds from the Side-winder at the rear tires. Both went flat and the car stalled.

Mark circled the blue Caddy at a hundred yards but drew no fire. Before he left civilization he had stopped at a minimart for a six-pack of beer. He wanted one right now, maybe it was still a little cold.

He sat in his car, watching the wounded luxury set of wheels. Nothing moved. Was it a standoff, or were they all dead or ready to give up? Mark moved closer, slowly. At fifty yards he circled the Caddy again in his Ford, using it like a horse in a Wild West movie. Again he saw no life. He edged closer and suddenly the side he was nearest exploded with gunfire from at least two weapons. Mark dove for the floor and, when he worked his way out the other side of the car, he knew his steed was mortally wounded. Both tires on the other side went flat, and he felt several large rounds hit the hood and engine.

Mark worked his way to the trunk, got it open

without drawing fire, and pulled out his arms suitcase. Just as he remembered, he hadn't brought a long gun—no Stoner, no rifle, not even the Mossburg. He looked at the M-3 fraggers. A couple of them might persuade anybody left in the car to give up.

Mark took the fragmentation grenades, pulled the pin on one, and lobbed it toward the Caddy. It was a hundred and fifty feet and the small bomb sailed within fifty feet of the car before it hit and exploded with a cracking roar. There was no reaction from those in the car.

Mark shouted at the men.

"You want some more of that? Give up and live for a while. I can blow you to hell if you stay inside there. Come out now with your hands up and no weapons."

There was no response. Mark took the Sidewinder and two fraggers and darted toward a rock twenty yards ahead between him and the Caddy. It was three feet high and twice that wide, offering a good fighting position. He gained the rock with no fire, and peered over it. This time he knew he could get the bomb to the car, but he didn't want to kill them. He still wanted Jerele alive so he could talk to him. Tactically before, he knew he had used the machine gun too much; he could have killed Jerele. But at the time it had been a defensive action as well as offensive. Now he could afford to be more careful, more selective. If Jerele were still alive in that blue Caddy, Mark was determined to keep him alive until he could make him talk.

Mark threw another grenade with intent and accuracy. He placed it just to the rear of the blue car, figuring the blast would shake up the men but not hurt them. The green bomb landed within three feet of where he wanted it, but too close to the car's gas tank. Some of the shrapnel went into the tank and the sparks from the metal provided the ignition. The gas tank didn't explode, but the gasoline splashed into the sand and whooshed up into flames, engulfing the back of the car.

Mark heard screams from the Caddy and a moment later both doors on the far side opened. Two figures ran into the desert, back toward the trees where Mark had been.

One man was short, fat, and ran slowly. Mark hurried after them, skirting the burning car, and once around it sent a shot over the men's heads.

"Stop or I'll kill you!" Mark thundered.

The shorter man fell to the ground, panting. The other turned sideways in the classic dueler's pose and began firing a handgun. Mark lifted the Sidewinder and fired. Two rounds hit the other man in the chest and neck, and he went down, his arms flopping wildly as he tried to continue shooting. He curled in the sand and then attempted to sit up. He lifted the .45 once more, and realized how heavy it was but held it in the air until his eyes glazed and his heart made its final desperate surge to supply blood, which only rushed out onto the sand of Arizona. He fell back into a nest of small cactus as he died.

Mark came up slowly. The short man sat up with difficulty, shaded his eyes from the sun, and a strange smile lit his face.

"Well, Mr. Scott, here we are at last, face to face."

Mark recognized the voice. He squatted, the Sidewinder in his right hand. He frisked Victor Jerele and found no weapon.

"Mr. Jerele, I believe. You and I have some talking to do. Are you comfortable? Could I have the waiter bring you a bourbon on the rocks? You're going to need it."

"No, I have to watch my weight." He smiled.

"Beautiful day, don't you think? Perhaps it will get a bit warmer in the upper deserts."

"Jerele, what happens August tenth, this Sunday?"

"So that's all you know. Good. You haven't made much progress, have you?"

"Jerele, how much do you know about the desert?"

"I've lived in Phoenix for three years."

"But have you ever spent any time out here?"

"Well . . ."

"You're lucky it isn't a hot day. But even today it will get so hot that your tongue will stick to the roof of your mouth, your lips will crack, your nose will feel like you're rubbing it inside with sandpaper with every breath, and your lungs will scream and refuse to accept that hot air you keep giving them. Then wait until it really gets hot and your water is all gone. How much water did you bring, Victor?"

Jerele looked at the dead man a few feet from him.

"You killed Wilson."

"True, Jerele. It was him or me. This time it was him, just like in the Wild West days out here a hundred years ago. Only the weapons and the clothes have changed. Maybe the reasons as well. What makes a man die for somebody else like that? What happens Sunday, Jerele, when you shut down the whole country's communications system?"

Jerele's head jerked up. He couldn't help the reaction.

"How the hell do you know that?"

"It's not a very hard guess. Now what happens while the wires are down? A series of bank heists, stealing some atom bombs from an SAC base? Taking over a missile-launching base? Trying to blow up Washington? What's behind it all?"

"Hell, how should I know? He gives me orders, I

82

follow them. Now we better get in your car and drive back to town before I get a sunburn. My skin is sensitive."

"It's pink already, Jerele, and we can't drive anywhere. *If* we go, we walk. Your hoods killed my Ford."

"Just a flat tire or two."

"Much more than that, Jerele. They blew apart the oil lines or the brake lines, and she's dead in the water." Mark didn't know this for sure, but it could be true.

"Hey, don't say that. Let's go look."

Mark fired a .45 round between the man's spread legs as he started to get up.

"Stay, Jerele. You aren't moving a step until you tell what else is happening Sunday and who's going to do it. Savvy?"

Jerele looked up at Mark and snorted. "Fuck off, bastard, I'll never tell you a thing."

"Suit yourself, sit there and fry in the sun." Mark sat down in the sand across from Jerele. "It's nearly one o'clock. We've got another six hours of sunshine. How is that forehead of yours going to feel then?"

Jerele looked up but didn't reply. He had been sitting so his back was to the sun. His short-sleeved shirt exposed his arms now, and he hugged them across his stomach in the shadow of his body.

"You stay right where you are, Jerele. I'm going to look at the Ford."

"The forest service will be here shortly," Jerele said. "I hear they always check out a smoke, and this is a big smoke in an unknown location." Jerele looked up, excited now. "They'll be coming in a big chopper and see we're in trouble and land. Then that gun of yours won't do you any good and I'll charge you with murder."

Mark shook his head. "No way, José. There's

nothing to burn out here. The forest service won't even bother with a little smudge like this. They might think it could be a downed plane, but they'll check with the airport and get a negative there. I don't think you better plan on being rescued by the forestry people." The car fire was almost burned out; the rear seats had been smoldering and smoking, but now had almost finished.

Mark had thought of the smoke danger, but dismissed it. He didn't think they would investigate a smoke in this area where there was nothing to sustain a grass fire. Anyway there was nothing he could do about it. If they came, they came. He thought his logic was sound on the smoke. If it had been a worry to forestry, they would have had a spotter there before now.

Mark again ordered Jerele to stay where he was and walked back to the Ford. He wanted a beer. Anything liquid to keep up his strength.

At the Ford he looked under the hood first. All seemed fine until he checked the distributor cap. At least one round had hit it. The whole plastic cap was shattered, the plug wires sticking out at odd angles. There was no way the car would run until it had a new cap.

He went to the driver's door and got in. So much for the Ford. His hand moved to the six-pack of beer and tore a can from the plastic holder. It seemed strangely light. It was empty. He checked the rest. A slug had gone through the door and hit the cans. Four of the last five were empty, making a wet stain on the seat. He took the last can of beer and drank it slowly. It was warm, bitter but wet. When it was gone he thought about the walk out.

Not before dark, and coolness. First he had to get into the shade. He'd even take Jerele with him. That was the reasonable, logical thing to do. Still they might not make it. They were at least ten miles from the highway into this strip of no-man's-land, and it was far from a heavily traveled route. Mark thought about it as he walked back to the spot where Jerele still sat.

He could make Jerele think that they were going to walk out right now. Get him so frightened and physically spent that he would tell everything he knew just to stay alive—to have help in staying alive. Yes, Jerele would crack.

Mark stopped and stared down at the man sitting in the sand.

"You heard me try to start the Ford? It doesn't. Your bullets smashed up the engine and it won't run without a new distributor cap, and the one off your Cadillac won't fit."

"By God, let me go look!"

Mark nodded and let him get up. Jerele walked stiff-legged and awkwardly as he plowed through the sand and rocks to the Ford. He stared at the distributor then back at Mark.

"Hell, you broke that with a rock."

Mark showed the other man the scrapings of lead on the broken plastic.

"Sure I broke it. I want to walk fifteen miles through the desert on the hottest August day on record. I'm stone dumb, that's what I am."

"Walk out? What the hell you mean?" Jerele asked.

"Just what I said. If you want to get out of here you walk out. I hope you're good at hiking, Jerele."

"I can't walk out of here. Asthma. It hurts me to take two deep breaths. Why the hell you suppose I moved to Phoenix?"

"That doesn't matter now, does it? Now we either live or we die, depending how clever and how strong we are. Do you feel either clever or strong right now, Victor Jerele? You realize you probably won't live until Sunday, don't you? You never will

85

see the fruits of all your work to pull off this communications blackout."

"I won't live until Sunday? Of course I will. Why wouldn't I?"

"Because, little man, I'm bigger than you are. I have a gun, and I'm not going to let you get all the way out of here even if you try."

Mark motioned to him. "Come on, we might as well get started. At least we can walk back to some trees, maybe we can rest there and cool off a little before we move on." Mark put the .45 back in its holster on his belt.

"Mr. Scott, you are wrong. I'm not walking, you are, and you're going to carry me."

Mark started to laugh, then looked down at the short man, and all he could see were the twin muzzles of a .45 caliber derringer, pointing directly at his heart.

Chapter 7

ONE DOWN, AND ONE OUT

Those two .45 barrels leering at him looked awesome. It had been a long time since Mark had stared at possible violent death quite so closely. The small fat man holding the gun grinned and ran his fingers through his shoulder-length blond hair.

"Now, the shoe is on the other foot, Mr. Scott. The first thing I want you to do carefully—oh, so very gently and carefully—is to take that .45 automatic out of your holster and lay it in the sand. Then back up three long steps. You'll still be in easy range for my little double shooter here, that you'd better believe. Do it now!"

Mark had no choice. He took the automatic out and put it on the sand. Wait, he would wait for a better time. Just be patient and wait. He stood and stepped back three times.

Jerele came forward, groaned as he bent over his big belly to pick up the .45 and pushed off the safety. Then he laughed.

"Now, Mr. Scott, you fix up that Ford, wire it together, paste it up, but make it work."

Mark shook his head. "It doesn't matter who has the .45, Jerele, that distributor is shattered and it would take a miracle if it held together long enough even to start the engine. And that's if I had some ducting tape or something else to paste all the pieces of plastic back together. No way. The car won't run, you'll have to accept that. Try to fix it yourself if you want to."

"I'm not mechanical. So it's a long walk. You'll have to carry me."

"That's not using your head, Jerele. In this heat I'd give out in a mile. We've got fifteen miles to cover. You're too fat. You must go a hundred and ninety pounds. I can't carry you very far."

"Goddamnit, Scott, you are going to try. And remember, I've got this .45 right in your ear. If you can't carry me out of here, you're no more use to me, and a threat. So if you want to live, you pick me up and carry me. Now let's do it!"

Mark shrugged, his mind churning. It might work out better this way. He could stumble, fall. He worked on that and other ideas. He got down on one knee with his back to Jerele.

"Climb on my back, but I can't take you very far. I'm as dried out as you are."

"Shut up and pick me up and let's move," Jerele said.

Mark did.

Fifteen minutes later they were approaching a half dozen trees no more than ten feet high growing up in a wash near the road. Jerele had insisted they walk off the road to them.

"We'll get lost out here and never find our way if we don't stay near the road," Mark said.

Jerele used his only argument: the muzzle of Mark's own .45 pressed harder into his ear. Jerele was careful. He made Mark stop, then drop to one knee and let him off Mark's back. Mark rolled over in the shade on his back and relaxed. He had to show great fatigue. Actually he felt little different from normal. Carrying a one-hundred-eighty-pound man for a mile wasn't easy, but his desert workouts had kept him in top physical trim.

"Christ, Jerele, I'm worn out. I can't go another step. You've got to find yourself a new horse."

A .45 round slammed into the ground six inches from Mark's head as the gun roared its message. Mark counted silently. Three, that was the third round fired from the .45's total of eight.

"Scott. Shut up and do what I say. When I say get up, you get up. This shade is damned nice, now, isn't it? We'll stay here for a while. Maybe until the sun goes down; then I'll be cooler and I can walk a little and rest my horse. That's all you are now, Scott, a goddamned horse that's gonna get me out of here, and then I shoot you. You got that?"

Mark didn't respond. The .45 spoke again and rocks splattered against his boot. Mark jumped, sat halfway up, a response he knew Jerele wanted.

"What? Huh? I must have dozed off, passed out. So damn tired, bushed. Carrying you was murder. Why don't you lose about eighty pounds?" Through it all Mark was counting. That was four rounds spent. Jerele had only four more rounds left in the automatic.

"Don't try to con me, Scott. You're strong as a damn mule. You never even stumbled or paused or rested on that hike. You're doing just fine. Keep on doing it that way and you stay alive."

Mark let his disgust for Jerele creep on his face. He couldn't play it too weak-kneed, or Jerele would suspect something.

"You aren't going to shoot me, Jerele. Not until you can see the highway and know damn well you

89

can get to it. And we've got a long way to go before then." Mark sat up slowly, one hand raised in a caution and quiet sign. He spoke in a whisper now. "Jerele, don't move, there's a six-foot rattlesnake right behind you. He was crawling by, but now he's coiled; he could strike at any time."

"You're lying," Jerele said softly without moving.

"Want to bet your stupid life on it?"

"What's he doing now?"

"Just sitting there, head weaving back and forth, watching you. He'd have a good strike at your back or your thigh. He's about two feet from you now and coiled."

"Jesus, what should I do?"

"Pray a lot. Your only chance is to freeze for about ten minutes until he decides you're just another tree and he leaves."

"No way! I've got to move; my back is killing me."

"Then roll this way fast. Dive and roll and come up shooting behind you. He won't follow you; he'll be afraid of you once you're away from his strike length."

"You're conning me, Scott. Hell, I'd try the same thing in your place."

"Okay, have it your way. Snakebit you'll still have maybe a fifty-fifty chance of living. I'd have to cut you and bleed you a lot, try to get the poison out. Course that would weaken you and you couldn't be moved or anything. I'd have to go out and bring in some help. Hell, I might forget my way or have a few beers first, know what I mean?"

Mark watched Jerele's face. He was frozen into a curious mask of terror, hatred, and anger. The .45 still in his hand dipped slowly downward wavering from the weight of the weapon and the length of time he'd held it still.

Suddenly his face firmed, Jerele dove toward

90

Mark, rolled, and fired three shots behind him, then sat up in the dirt and brought the weapon back aimed at Mark.

"Nice try, Scott, but it didn't work. You had me going. You're good, lots of spirit, reminds me of me fifteen years ago. Only I never got caught with my pants down this way. Okay, I guess I shouldn't have believed you about that snake. On your feet, move it over next to that scrub oak. Take off your belt and throw it on the ground behind you."

Mark moved carefully, not sure what was going to happen, but knowing now that Jerele had only one more round in the magazine. All the other spare rounds were in the suitcase with the other weapons back by the dead Ford. Jerele hadn't thought to look for any more rounds. The Sidewinder SMG was back there somewhere too. Somebody was going to find a bonanza when they discovered that suitcase and the chatter gun.

Mark took off his leather belt with a heavy buckle on it and threw it behind him. Jerele picked it up and backed Mark against a three-inch-thick tree trunk, then wrapped the belt around both tree and Mark and pulled it up so tight Mark wasn't sure he could breathe. The buckle was at the back of the tree.

"Now your hands, smart ass. Hold them in front of you."

Mark found he could breathe after all. He put out his hands and watched as the short man tied them with strips of cloth he tore from his handkerchief. The Penetrator looked down at his hands, then at the short man with the long blond hair who had just tied them.

"You know something about knots, don't you?"

"Flattery will do you no good now. I think I'll just lie down over there in the shade. Take a small nap and when I wake the sun will be down and

91

then, with the cooler air, I'll be able to ride you all the way out to the road. I'm not so dumb I don't know where I am, Scott."

He stared at Mark for a moment, then shrugged. "Frankly I was trying to decide whether I should take you with me or leave you here with a bullet in your brain. Anytime I have you near me you're a threat, and I would want to stop and rest along the way again." He lifted his hands in an unknowing gesture, palms up. "Hell, I'll decide when I wake up. I might be feeling more charitable than I am now."

Jerele went a dozen yards away to a bigger tree with more shade and stretched out on the hard ground. He turned twice and at last found a comfortable spot.

Mark watched him and when he heard the long, even breathing usually associated with sleeping, Mark figured it was safe to try to undo the cloth wrappings. With his teeth working on the cloth the knots would mean nothing. He would tear through the soft cotton cloth easily. That's why he almost laughed when Jerele tied him with the handkerchief. But he had to be sure Jerele was sleeping first.

Mark called softly, using Jerele's name. Then he called louder, and saw the man stir, throw out one hand, draw it back, and mumble something. Yes, Mark decided, it was real sleep. Jerele had been exhausted by the day's trip and the fight and then the move up here, even though he had been carried.

Mark attacked the strips of cloth around his wrists. In less than a minute he had them ripped off and his hands were tugging at the belt, sliding it around the tree. He had the buckle almost where he could reach it when Jerele suddenly sat up, lifted his hand, and shouted, "We're number one! We're number one!" Then he laughed, lay back down, and continued to sleep. A dream.

Mark tugged at the belt again, caught the buckle and pulled it in front, then quickly undid the fastener and moved away from the tree. He threaded the belt back through his pant loops and buckled it as he stared at Jerele. The .45 lay near the small man's right hand. Mark needed it, and he had to find the derringer as well. Strange that he had missed it before. Jerele must use a crotch holster.

The Penetrator moved toward Jerele without rustling a leaf or brushing a twig or frightening an ant. He picked up the .45 then slapped Jerele sharply in the face.

"What . . . what . . .?" Jerele came awake, his hand clawing the sand for the .45.

"Welcome to sunny Arizona, Mr. Jerele. We hope you'll enjoy your sunburn. Now, carefully dig out that derringer, and remember, I'd just as soon shoot you as spit in your face. Oh, I won't make it easy, it'll hurt a lot. A .45 slug through a knee is supposed to be the most painful gunshot wound possible. The derringer!"

Jerele shook with anger. He was livid, his fury turning his sunburned face even redder.

"How did you get free? How? I had you tied good."

"The derringer."

Slowly Jerele reached past his belt, down the fly of his pants inside toward his crotch, and brought out the small weapon, holding it by the grips.

Mark took it, broke it open, checked the two .45 rounds and put the weapon in his pocket.

"Now, Jerele. On your feet, we move. I've got an important meeting this afternoon, which means we've got to jog back to the highway and hitchhike a ride into town."

"Jog? Run? Are you out of your mind?" Jerele struggled to his feet, his face bathed in perspiration.

"You know I can't run, I can barely walk. Are you trying to kill me?"

"Not a bad idea, don't tempt me. Move out, in front, over to that track of a road and toward the highway. Move it!"

Mark kicked Jerele easily in the rear and he stumbled forward out of the shade into the burning sunshine.

They walked for half an hour. Jerele had fallen down twice. His face was a continuing red now, his eyes puffing.

"Water, Scott. For God's sake get me some water! This heat, this place. I can't stand much more of it."

Mark was hardly sweating. He had been cruising along behind Jerele, needing to poke him only occasionally with a finger stab on a kidney to keep him moving.

Jerele kicked a rock in the road, stumbled, and fell flat on his stomach in the dirt. One hand showed scratches that glowed red with new blood. Jerele got up to a sitting position.

"I'm not going a step farther," he said.

Mark walked past him a dozen feet. "Fine, Jerele. I'll tell them where to come look for your body. I'll be damned if I'm going to carry you."

"Just to some shade. There, a half mile. Those two big trees. Leave me there and I'll be fine for twenty-four hours. I'll give you fifty thousand dollars to get me out of here!"

Mark heard real fear creep into the man's voice. His face showed a fright so honest that he couldn't bluster or fake it, only say the words and let his soul hang out for anyone to see.

"I haven't got time, that appointment." Mark raised the .45 and walked back. "Maybe I should take pity on you and end it right here, quickly. I'd do as much for a good horse if it went down like this and couldn't get up."

Jerele held up his hands. "No! Oh God, no! Look, just half a mile. Help me over there and I'll give you a hundred thousand. I'm a rich man. I just made a half million dollars. I don't have it all yet but I'm getting it. I got a hundred thousand down, and the rest when it's all over. The whole hundred thousand is yours."

He was begging now, his reserves gone, his self-respect shattered.

"Scott! I can't mean that much to you. It's my life! Help me for Christ's sake. Haven't you got any feelings at all?"

"I have about as many as Marvin Butler had in Hollywood. You had him killed, didn't you? You blew him away because he was in your way."

Jerele pushed the glasses back on his nose and looked at Mark. "Would it make any difference if I said yes? He was in the way, we needed that union. Yes, he was killed, but it was an accident. He killed one of my men in the process. Now, I confessed, help me get into the shade!"

"Chicago, those sixty thousand phones, the white-phosphorous grenades. Did you set that up too?"

"Yes, yes, yes! And the stations. Now get me out of this stinking hellhole, out of this valley of death!"

"No."

Jerele couldn't believe it.

"No? You say you won't help me?"

"That's right." Mark turned and walked away. He heard Jerele struggling to his feet and following. Mark walked a quarter of a mile down the trail without looking back. He was moving slowly, but even so he could hear Jerele getting farther and farther behind. The road did not pass near any trees. Mark kept moving.

"Scott! Scott! Wait for me."

Mark turned and watched. Jerele was dragging one foot now; he couldn't pick it up. His breathing came through his mouth in gasps. His eyes were almost closed by swelling, and his forehead was layered with white water blisters from the sun. His ears were red, and both arms also had the white bumps of a blistering sunburn. Jerele's shirt was sweat-pasted to his skin and showed a dark, splotchy pattern. The short man wheezed now, and his breath came only in ragged gasps.

When he was ten feet from Mark, he stopped, swaying on unsteady legs, his hands out for balance.

"Scott, help me."

"Three men died trying to help you today, Jerele. You never even told them you were sorry or thanked them."

"I'm sorry, then. For Christ's sake, what do you want me to do? What torture do you want me to go through to pay for it? Do I have to heave out my guts on their bodies and cry over them?"

"That might help."

Jerele looked at Mark with slits for eyes through the puffing, and slowly he crumpled to the hot sand. He sat and tried to look up at Mark.

"Scott, what in hell do you want. What *is* important to you? Not . . . money . . ." He was having trouble talking now, his words running together.

Mark watched him and realized Jerele was close to passing out from sunstroke.

"One thing I want, then I'll help you," Mark said. "What happens Sunday during the blackout, and who are you working for?"

"Christ, easy. Nothing you can do about it." He tried to swallow. His tongue was twice as large as it had been. Jerele looked up at Mark.

"What's happening . . . don't know. Gen. Richard Hollingsworth Hemphill. Brigadier. Commands Edwards Air Force Test Facility. Damned if I know what . . . trying to do. I deliver blackout on schedule Sunday morning."

Jerele fell forward on his hands and knees and looked up at Mark.

Mark stared at him. There was no possibility the man was lying. He was at the end of his strength, a deathbed confession. He wasn't strong enough to lie now.

"For this you had how many men killed? For this you blew up towers and the Chicago switching stations, and I can only guess how many more you are going to kill when you blow up facilities and black out transmissions Sunday. And all this for money, for a hundred thousand dollars?"

"More, much more . . . after . . . done."

"But if we don't get out of here, you won't live to see any of that money, Jerele. Have you been thinking about that?"

Tears streaked down the man's dusty face. He tried to wipe them away and as he did he fell flat on the sand. Jerele used much of his remaining strength to get to a sitting position.

"Now, help me. You promised. You promised!"

"Jerele, I don't make deals with murderers, with contemptible scum like you. What do you expect me to do, carry you out of here? We'd both be buzzard bait within two hours. I could help you. I could put a .45 slug through your brain."

Jerele shook his head. "No, help. Promised!"

"You don't understand yet, do you Jerele? When you shot up my car back there, you signed your death warrant. Ten miles in this heat is impossible for you. At night, maybe, but not today. Not even now. You're drained, you've cashed in your chips. This is the last hour of your life on this earth."

Mark held the .45 aimed at the man's head; then he sighed and sat down in front of him. "Are you still rational? You're going into sunstroke at any minute. You'll be unconscious for a while and out of your head. Your body gets so hot it cooks your brain and you die and it isn't easy. You'll wake up and hurt like hell for about an hour."

Mark hit the release button and took the magazine from the automatic. There were no rounds left in it. He pulled the slide back and caught the live round extracted from the chamber. Mark laid the three items on the ground three feet in front of Victor Jeerle.

"Now, this is your decision. You can stay here and take your chances with the heat and the snakes. Or you can put this round in the magazine and put it in the .45 and have one round ready to fire. You can keep the weapon and try to get to some shade. Or when it gets too bad, and you know you can't live very long, and the pain is unbearable, you can put the muzzle in your mouth and blow the top of your head off. It's a clean, quick way."

Victor Jerele stared at Mark through the slit eyes, and Mark didn't know if he were still rational.

"Jerele, do you understand? I can't save you. I must get up to Edwards and try to stop whatever this air force man is going to try. I couldn't save you now no matter what I did. I have no responsibility to save a killer for the gas chamber. It's better this way. Do you understand?"

Jerele nodded. His mouth and tongue wouldn't work. His eyes were shut.

"Can you reach the weapon?"

Jerele nodded again.

Mark had pinpointed the nearest shade. It was three hundred yards across a small wash. He pointed. "Shade, to your right, try for it if you want to."

More tears came from the slitted eyes.

Mark touched his shoulder. Jerele's sagging head came up, his eyes more alert.

"Don't waste the round trying to shoot me. I'll be well out of range by the time you get the automatic loaded. Do you understand? Use it however you want to, but don't waste it trying for me."

Mark stood, turned, and walked down the road. He didn't look back. He heard the magazine go into the handle when he was about a hundred yards away. Then he estimated the time Jerele would need to pull the slide. He might be too weak to do it now. There was no shot. Mark walked faster now, long strides, wanting to run, but knowing he had lost too much strength and fluids to run for long. Usually he could cover eight miles in fifty minutes. But walking it would take him two hours now, *if* he could make it. Mark came to the top of a small rise and turned to look back. Victor Jerele sat in the same place in the road. Mark thought he could see the weapon raised, but he wasn't sure.

The booming explosion of the .45 in the silently thin desert air jolted Mark. He saw the body below him jerk and flop from side to side. Mark watched closely and at last there was no more movement.

The Penetrator turned and stretched out with new determination. He had to get to Edwards Air Force Base as quickly as he could. Now all he had to do was defeat time and distance and eight more miles of desert and the 110-degree heat with no water and no transport, only with his muscles, his mind and his determination.

Chapter 8

A WALK IN THE SUN

Mark thought no more about Victor Jerele. The world was a better place without him. Jerele had paid the price for his actions. Now, Mark concentrated on the stretch of road ahead. He had slowed his pace after the rise in the trail where he had seen Jerele kill himself.

Beyond he could see a winding flatness that looked at least two miles long. There were occasional cactus now, some large ones, and Mark kept watching for the barrel cacti he was so familiar with from the California deserts. The barrel could be cut open to find water, of a kind, and, while not appetizing, it often afforded enough moisture to save a dying man. Mark kept watching.

But this was a different area; a different set of plants grew here. If he got dry enough he could drink the blood of a rabbit, if he could catch one or shoot it.

Mark felt his mouth drying out. He kept walking,

trying to maintain a four-mile-an-hour gait, but not sure at all if he were holding that pace.

Think of something else! Think of something good. Mark concentrated on his *sho-tu-ca* powers, knowing full well that part of the value of the ancient Cheyenne medicine was the psychology of it, the willing of his body to do what he wanted it to. But now he was not sure if the special powers could help him overcome the traumatic physical draining of his body fluids. He had no pain center to block, no area on which he could concentrate.

At last he thought of swimming and playing in a mountain lake high in the Sierra Nevada, where the water was fifty degrees and so refreshing it took his breath away. He was splashing in it—swimming, fishing, boating, diving off the boat into the coolness, then stretching out under the pine trees in the shade to warm up before he stormed back into the cold water.

Mark thought about the lake for another mile, and found himself again at a small rise as the road curved around the valley and he hoped headed for the highway.

Then he fell. He lay on the hot sand looking at a small red ant carrying a piece of food much larger than itself, trudging along toward the ant hole.

"Get up," Mark said aloud. "Get up and walk or you die here in the desert with the others. Get up and walk!" All at once it seemed that his energy was gone, his body drained, his will to survive even in question. He stared at the ground for what seemed like a full minute; then he rolled to his right and pushed upward.

Mark stood, swayed back and forth a moment, then moved forward. Something bothered him. What was it? Now even his mind was starting to fail him. No it was his voice, that was it. He could not hear the words he said. He knew he had spoken them out loud. He tried again but felt his swollen tongue lolling in his mouth and knew it could not move the way it should to help form the words.

Water! He had to have some soon to survive. Mark looked around for a dark spot where a spring might be found near the surface. There was none. His glance followed the wash nearest him, but there was no sign of any wetness along its entire length. Nothing but sand and rocks, lizards, small wild flowers, occasional scrub brush and trees and, of course, snakes, though he spied none at the moment.

Another step down the road. Mark looked back up the trail and realized his steps were now half as long as they had been an hour ago. He looked at his watch. Yes, it had been an hour since he had left Jerele. How far had he come? Not four miles, he knew that for certain.

Mark stared hard ahead. Down the road . . . move on down the road. He had to keep walking. He couldn't run so he had to walk. Mark reached in his pocket and came out with the derringer. Angrily he started to throw it into the desert. Silly. That was stupid. He might need the little gun. But he didn't want to carry anything he didn't have to. Still he kept it. His shirt—should he strip it off? No, it helped keep him cool, amounted to a place for evaporation of his sweat, and protected him from the blistering sun. How could it be so hot this time of the year? He shook his head and took another step. His continued existence right now depended on his taking another step. He had to move on down the road.

Was this how the Penetrator's story was going to end? Was he going to die here in the desert and no one ever know what happened to him?

"Hell no!" Mark shouted. It came out only as a gurgle of unintelligible sounds.

That scared him. He looked at the edges of the

103

trail again, watching for the round, thorny barrel cactus. He'd settle for even a small one right now. One that might have a cup of fluid inside its prickly skin. But there were none.

One more step down the road.

Ahead he saw still another rise in the trail, maybe the length of a long city block away. That was the goal: he knew he had to have many small victories now. He had to set objectives he could reach and never fail. If he failed to reach one of his objectives, he might lose the battle, and lose the whole war.

He imagined machine gun chattering on the left; he made a down sign with his hand, and the whole platoon hit the dirt in the steaming underbrush of the Vietnam jungle. Suddenly there were no other sounds. The insects, the birds, everything had gone silent. Mark lifted himself and looked across the small clearing ahead of them; he saw only a stream and a village. It had to be a Cong hideout. Probably they were all sympathizers with the Viet Cong. They would smile and sell food to the Americans during the day and then at night they would gun them down, blow them up, jam them full of bamboo spears tipped with cow dung. Goddamned dirty Cong!

Mark ran with the first squad to the right. Running low, they got to the edge of the water and hid behind trees. The third squad raced to positions upriver. Then he wormed his way through the wetness of the jungle floor and watched the second squad get into position behind any cover they could find. A lone Vietnamese woman left one of the huts and walked toward the small bridge crossing the stream. She was about to step on it when someone screamed at her from another hut. She became excited, frightened, turned around and suddenly ran onto the bridge.

The bamboo-and-rope bridge blew into a thousand splintering pieces, and as it went the Cong opened fire from the huts. Mark and the other men returned fire and threw grenades. In five minutes the Cong had retreated from the village, leaving the headman of the little community hanging in one of the huts with bamboo splinters driven into each eye and through both ears, then a dozen more planted through his heart. His wife had also been killed.

The medic patched up two of the men who had been wounded. The lieutenant put out security front and back and began the march back to base camp. It was one hell of a way to fight a war, with no front lines, no known enemy, hit-and-run patrols you couldn't find when you wanted to. Mark stepped into the three-foot-deep river and waded across.

As he watched the stream, it slowly vanished from in front of his eyes and turned into a desert track of a road through Arizona, with a small wash extending across it, and a scrub pine to one side.

How long had he been out of his mind, dreaming about Vietnam again? At least he had kept walking, kept marching, like that time . . . No. No. Here and now. Not back then and over there. He was here in Arizona, and he was going to die of thirst and exposure unless he did every damned thing right! And that didn't include hallucinating and dreaming about war or cold places!

Another step along the road.

That's what it was all about. Another step and then another one and he moved forward. The small rise was just in front of him now and he saw larger hills beyond that. Were they the mountains? Had he walked the wrong way on the road, taking him deeper and deeper into the hills? He wasn't sure. He stopped moving and listened. Perhaps he could hear the sound of a car or truck on the highway if it really were in this direction.

He heard nothing.

Mark wiped one dirty hand across his sweaty face, then plodded on ahead. At least he could still move; he was walking. His steps were shorter again, his pace unsure, but he was forging ahead.

The Penetrator knew he had to keep walking. He couldn't afford to drift into another fantasy or start hallucinating again.

Another step down the road.

Yes, better, that was better, and when he got to the highway, he would lay down on the center stripe and wait for a car or a truck or even a motorcycle to come along. Maybe he'd be lucky and find a motor home with a cold beer in the refrigerator and a soft bed he could sleep in.

Mark jerked himself awake. His eyes had closed for a few seconds. But he had kept marching, just like basic training. He had to stay awake. If he went to sleep now he would wake up and find himself dead.

Sweat dripped off his chin in oily, dirty drops. Plan, plan ahead, plan to walk, and walk.

Another step along the road.

Yes. And when he got back to Phoenix he would get a taxi to his hotel and rest and not drink too much at first, rest and soak in a cold tub and then take a shower and drink ice water, sipping it at first and then, after a few hours, he'd drink gallons!

His eyes blurred and he thought he saw a small airplane. Then Mark realized he did. It was coming closer, but it was too high. No one up there would see him. They would not expect to find a lone man walking through this hellhole, and they would not be watching for anything below. They were just passing over. That's what he liked to do best in Arizona, just pass over or through most of it quickly.

Keep walking. Keep walking.

The trail twisted again to the right, and now he saw that it was a definite road, with twin tire tracks and only a few weeds grown up in the middle. Yes! He remembered the road looked this way closer to the highway.

He looked again. The road climbed now. Hadn't he dropped down off the highway when he turned away from the blacktop? He thought so. A new feeling of confidence surged through Mark. Now he was getting there! Now he was going to make it. He blinked to get his eyes clear, then walked ahead with more power, with more confidence, knowing he was going to make it.

Then he stumbled and fell. He never saw the small stone that tripped him. It had been enough to upset his delicate balance and dropped him into the rocks and sand of the roadway. Mark sat up and blinked rapidly. He was trying to clear his eyes, he told himself, but the joy and confidence of a few moments ago were gone, washed away by the failure of his body. He couldn't even walk right!

The thought pounded at him, drove him down, tried to keep his spirits from rising.

The Penetrator got to one knee and fought down a mounting panic. He would not go over the edge. He would not fall apart the way Victor Jerele had. He was stronger, had more guts, had a better-trained mind than that. Nothing could defeat him. No one. Thousands had tried. Now was no time to let his own mind turn him into a blubbering failure, and a dead man at the same time. To fail here was to die!

He surged upward off his knee and stood, wobbled a little, then took another step down the road.

Mark wanted to shout out in victory, to lift his finger indicating that he was number one.

Instead a small smile lit his grim face, breaking a coating of dust and dirt that had caked to the sweat, and gave way only to deep creases along cheeks and mouth.

Another step on the long road.

Mark was moving again, and in the right direction. He watched the next rise in the trail come closer and closer. Where were the damned barrel cacti? Never one around when you needed it, just like waitresses and pretty girls and cops.

The road twisted sharply now and he remembered. He wasn't more than a quarter of a mile off the highway. The car had been going too fast when he hit this corner and he almost lost control. Now he walked around the bend in the road at a cool two miles an hour and never faltered once.

Another step upon the road.

Mark had to concentrate on a fixed point ahead now and move directly toward it like a dancer making those spinning turns. Concentrate on the spot and not let go of it or he would go wandering all over the wide road. He picked a rock beside the edge of the path a hundred yards ahead as his objective and moved deliberately toward it, his jaw set in deadly determination. Each step took a conscious effort. He was glad there were no curbs here, because he would never have been able to lift his foot to get up them.

One more step.

The path narrowed. He came to his rock, and saw the next turn, and then another turn and then he stopped.

The sound came low and faint at first; then it grew and crept closer and louder until he could hear it plainly—the growling roar of a big truck powering down the hill toward town. He wasn't far from the highway! He was almost there!

Mark sensed a thrill rising in his throat that he

could never describe, but it was there. The thrill was like the emotions he felt sometimes but didn't know how to express, the swelling of pride and understanding and love and gratitude, the kind that choked him up so he couldn't talk.

Mark tried to walk faster. He coaxed his legs, urged his feet onward. He picked out his next goal, a small bush beside the road another hundred years ahead. Faster, longer steps now.

Then he fell again.

The ground simply came up fast and jolted his whole body. There was no rock to blame this time. He was trying too hard, trying to move too fast. Get up, dummy! Get up! Damn, he didn't want to move. It felt so good to lie there and not have to move, to lie there and not worry about the highway and high-walking.

Get up, stupid! You want to lie there in the dirt and die like a squashed rattlesnake on the blacktop? Get up!

Mark rolled over on his hands and knees. It took him a long time to get to a standing position, and when he did it was harder to move forward. Slowly now, a short step. He was shuffling the last few steps but he didn't care. He'd shuffle all the way to Buffalo if he had to. Yes, that's the spirit. Yes, that's the spirit. Keep moving.

Another damned step down the long road.

Another.

Another.

Mark came at last to his bush, and the road turned. Ahead up a slight rise no more than a hundred feet away he saw the edge of the blacktop. It was the road! He was nearly there!

The Penetrator stood for a moment, swaying, tears spilling down his cheeks, tears of joy, of gladness, of relief, of thanksgiving. Now he began to walk, lifting each foot high, placing it carefully ahead. He didn't want anyone to see him shuffling. (He would come into camp with some style after all!)

The high steps lasted to six; then he was back to a dragging shuffle, but he didn't realize it.

Another step.

"No, dummy, up, up the road." He walked and shuffled, his arms feeling like useless deadweight. He wished he could detach them and leave them behind. They weren't helping a damned bit.

Mark stopped, panting as the grade increased. He was just below the road level when a car slammed past. He could see only a part of the top. No help there.

More steps. Another step.

He struggled the last three yards up the steep gravel turnout until he came to the very edge of the blacktop. The highway here was straight for a hundred yards each way. Mark sat down on the very edge, nearly fell over backward, then righted himself. A man had to have some dignity.

Far down the road Mark sensed a vehicle coming. He wasn't sure if it were a car or a truck. He turned toward it but couldn't see anything. It was coming downhill heading into Carefree.

Then something began growing in the back of his consciousness, and it got larger and larger and hotter and hotter. Mark looked down the highway, but all he could see was a dark-red stain as the highway turned to a river of blood. He felt himself falling, but he didn't care. His hands flopped out uselessly in front of him, and instinctively cushioned part of his fall, as his face scraped onto the blacktop. Mark Hardin lay still.

He was dead. He knew he had to be dead. Nothing anywhere on earth could feel so pleasant, so wonderful. For a moment he didn't know what it was, then he sensed something cool, almost cold.

Mark shivered. It was such a weird sensation that he tried to laugh, but he couldn't.

There was a rumble of something that sounded like a voice, but it wasn't, and there was some kind of vibration and a low growling sound. Then everything faded and Mark returned to a soft, dreamy coolness that he wished could last forever.

Art Shaw watched the man in the Peterbilt sleeper cab behind him as he drove the 18-wheeler toward Carefree. He'd almost hit the guy, lying there on the edge of the highway. At least he didn't run over him. Out of his head, and way too full of fever. Art had bundled him up in a blanket filled with snow from the inside of his reefer trailer. That would cool him down, which is what the medicos would also do when they got a chance. He hoped he wouldn't have given the guy frostbite by the time they hit Carefree. He took the CB mike off the hook and pushed the SEND button.

"Breaker, breaker. Anybody in Carefree who can copy me? I've got a sick man in my sleeper and he needs help fast. This is Big Art. Over."

Shaw let up on the SEND button and waited for two minutes; then he sent the same message again. This time he got a response.

"Hey, Big Art, Rotten Apple here. I'm southbound into Carefree ahead of you. Don't think your signal will carry that far in these mountains. I'll do a 10-23 and see who I can dig up."

"Thanks, Rotten Apple. My patient's got sunstroke. Found him along the highway. No vehicle. Out like a light. I got him in his frosty underwear to cool him down. Go, good buddy."

"That's a Roger."

Art listened as Rotten Apple sent his message out, and from what he heard there was a response. Then Rotten Apple called Art.

"Hey, Big Art. We got a country doctor says he'll meet us at the Standard station with the county ambulance and see what he can do for your boy. What's your ETA Carefree?"

"About ten minutes, Rotten Apple."

"Good, I'm at about five. I'll see you there."

Art listened to the transmissions as Rotten Apple told Carefree their estimated time of arrival. Then he settled down slamming his Pete around the mountain roads with the forty-foot reefer behind him.

Mark's eyes felt glued shut. He didn't care; it was still cool. Mark didn't try to move, the coolness was invigorating. Was this death? He wasn't sure, but it felt so good he didn't want to know. Not right away. Then he remembered the desert and Victor Jerele and Edwards Air Force Base in California, and his eyes struggled to open. When they did he saw in an instant the white ceiling, the white walls, the white sheets, and the ugliest white nurse he had ever seen in a white uniform bending over him.

"Well, we finally woke up, didn't we, Buster? You should be dead, you know that? Walking around in the desert without any water, car, or anything. You just damned well should be dead. But you're strong as a mule and we pulled you through."

Something was bothering him. He felt better now that he knew he wasn't dead. He was sure he could get up and move if he had to, but he just lay still. He was cool, but he knew he should be doing something.

The time! The date!

He grabbed the woman's hand. "What day is this?" he asked, his words a little slurred but intelligible.

"Day? It's Saturday, has been all day. They

112

brought you in from Carefree yesterday. You're in Phoenix now, and you're going to stay here for another forty-eight hours. Doctor's orders."

"What time is it? Where's my wristwatch?"

"Time is 2:32 in the afternoon. Your watch is right there on the stand. And I've got four more rooms to check. Now you be a good boy and stay nice and quiet. Doctor says you're to be on a high-fluid intake for two more days. See that quart of orange juice? Drink it." She turned and went out the door.

Saturday afternoon! He'd lost a whole day. The blackout was set for tomorrow. He had to call Dan Griggs. He had to get out of there and on a plane to Los Angeles.

Mark tried to sit up. He made it on the second try. The room was fuzzy for a moment, then steadied. He grabbed the bottle of orange juice and drank half of it. He was still starved.

Mark flexed his arms, moved his legs. He could function. He felt his face and found a bandage over one eye and on his cheek. What was that for? He swung his legs over the side of the bed and paused, letting his head catch up. Then he drank the rest of the orange juice. For the next few minutes he was going to have to move fast and work hard. He hoped he could take it.

A half hour later he had found his clothes, dressed, slipped out of the hospital, and was in a taxi going to his motel. He would check out, mail a thousand dollars to the car rental agency to cover the damage to the rented Ford, and have plenty of time to catch the plane to Los Angeles. Then all he would have to do was figure out how to get to Edwards Air Force Base in time to do some good before Sunday.

Chapter 9

THIS IS A TEST EXERCISE

When Mark got to the airport and bought his ticket, he found he would have a two-hour wait for a plane to Los Angeles. He was a bit wobbly as he carried his one suitcase to the counter and checked it through. He had left one weapons suitcase in the desert and didn't want to go through the hassle of trying to check it through. He would find weapons he needed in California. He stopped at the restaurant and had a rare steak and another pint of orange juice. Mark wasn't sure which made him feel better.

He found a phone and called Dan Griggs collect.

"As soon as they said it was collect I knew it was from you, Mark. How the hell are you?"

"Fine, Dan, just fine. I've got a date for that big happening. It's set for tomorrow. I can't say when, but it involves all the commo lines in the country. They'll try for a total blackout. I don't know precisely when or why."

"Then those incidents a few days ago must have been a test and tomorrow it's for real," Dan said.

"Right. It has something to do with Edwards Air Force Base, the test facility outside of Los Angeles a way. I'll be there tonight and see what I can turn up."

"Do you have any names, Mark?"

"Only that it involves the base commander, a General Hemphill. Could you bottle him up somewhere?"

"A general? I can't go around slapping generals under arrest without some kind of proof. Anyway, this is Saturday, and I'd have to go through the Joint Chiefs and then . . ."

"Forget it. Just get word to the president that something is cooking. Maybe he'll have some ideas about what is going on."

"I'll try to contact him, Mark. He left this morning on a junket, one of those four-day crisscrossing-country trips. It's politic to show his colors, do some campaigning, get the pulse of the people."

"He won't be much help, but get word to him."

"Yes, if I can. I'll try to get through the Georgia Mafia that are clustered around him."

"Oh, one more thing you can do for me. Wire my credentials to the security office. Provost Marshal, Edwards Air force Base. Use the DOJ ID, Col. John Brown, special assignment, Justice. I want to have some clout when I get there if I can."

"Haven't you worn out that ID card yet, Mark? I never did ask you where you had that made, but it's better quality than we get. OK. I'll send the ID and ask for total cooperation."

"Fine. I don't even know what I'm looking for out there, but I'll charge in and try. What could that base commander be planning that would necessitate a news blackout?"

"Phone him now and ask him."

116

"You're a bundle of laughs, Dan. You probably will hear what happens. Thanks for the help."

They said good-bye and hung up; then Mark had a long drink of water. He couldn't remember when his body had been so dried out; otherwise he felt fine. The doctor told him that he had a mild case of dehydration and a touch of sunstroke, but the snow blanket had kept his body temperature from reaching the fatal point. No, the doctor couldn't have told him that; he never talked directly to a doctor. It came back to him slowly. It had been a conversation between the doctor and nurse when he had been almost unconscious, but not quite.

He went to the men's room and took a better look at the bandage on his face. The injury was where he dove into the blacktop. Mark peeled off the tape and checked. A dozen scratches that had started to heal. They might look a lot less noticeable than a half-bandaged face. He went to the emergency first aid station in the airport and had the duty nurse put some disinfectant on the scrapes, and when she was done the abrasions were sealed off from the air, while he didn't look like a monster from outer space. That treatment would have to last for a while.

Mark read the newspaper, and then walked to the passenger gate, being the first one in line when the loading ramp door opened.

An hour later in Los Angeles, he rented a car and drove north to Burbank, then on out Interstate 5 to San Fernando, where he took State Highway 14 north to Lancaster, then to Rosamond, and in at the west gate of the sprawling air force base. His ID was checked and quickly approved, and he drove on to the base headquarters.

He went directly to the air police office and asked to see the ranking officer on duty, who turned out to be a young second lieutenant named McCafferty who was sharp and eager, but of no real help.

"Lieutenant, is General Hemphill on the base?"

"Yes, sir. I believe he is, sir. However, directing people is not part of our function here."

"Lieutenant, I didn't ask your function. Direct me to his residence."

The lieutenant hesitated.

"You *do* know where the general is quartered on base, do you not, Lieutenant?"

"Oh, yes sir. Yes I do. But I don't believe the general would be there now."

"Oh?"

"No sir. This is Saturday night, and I believe the general would be playing bingo at the officer's club. He always plays on Saturday night, sir, and he's good at it. He can handle twenty cards at once."

"You don't say. When does the bingo game end?"

"About eleven, sir."

"Thanks. Now, is there a transit BOQ that I could use for a few hours?"

That the officer could arrange, and a half hour later, Mark lay down and took a nap. Nothing would happen until after the bingo game, he was sure of that. He'd get some rest and be ready to go by midnight. But go where? Do what?

In Air Force One high over the piney hills of Georgia, Sgt. Lew Grout sat at the communications console of the big plane. The array of lights and dials and intricate pieces of radio and related equipment took up space a dozen feet long and half the width of the plane. Part of his responsibility was to monitor the equipment, watch for any malfunction or problem and take care of any other minor failure as they flew. Many of the systems had double backups, and he had to check those functions too.

High over Georgia, in the darkness of midnight,

Sergeant Grout made some intricate repairs to several of the panels. One touch of a certain line switch and half the whole system would short out and destroy itself.

But it wasn't time yet, not nearly time yet. He had his orders exactly what to do, and the promise of a large bonus if all went right. Sergeant Grout had never seen ten thousand dollars in a stack in his life, but he had now been promised that much. He'd get it in one-dollar bills and stack them in a suitcase, go home, and just sit there and look at them at night!

He stretched and watched the dials. All A-One so far, and it would stay that way. He was on duty until after eight in the morning and by then they would be far to the west, perhaps even near California. He didn't have a time target; it was more a question area. When they got to the right place he would touch that one line switch and the inside of the commo room would zap itself into a mass of junk.

Grout sat there watching the dials and reading a paperback at the same time. He would be done with the book well before dawn. Then what would he do? After every five pages he took another reading on the mass of dials and readouts in front of him. Nothing would go wrong. He was sure of that. All he had to do was check on their location and watch for China Lake.

Mark Hardin had changed his plans, gone to the bingo game, and had a monitor point out General Hemphill to him. True enough, the one-star was playing twenty hard cards, and even as Mark watched, the general filled in a double postage-stamp card and shouted "Bingo" so loud the caller jumped, dropped the ball, and had to scramble to find it to check out the general's card for the fifty-dollar prize.

The night of bingo ended without a blackout game, where all the squares must be covered. The general didn't win the five-hundred-dollar prize. The men and women quickly cleared the hall.

Mark followed the general to his car, where his driver had been waiting. The general and his lady were helped into the car, and driven sedately away. Mark stayed well back, and saw the big car, with the general's flags flying, swing into the commander's official residence behind two gates and three screens of shrubbery and trees.

The general had shown no nervousness. He was not as tall as Mark—heavier, but still trim, and wore his casual suit with a flair. Thinning red hair showed his freckles and a nose that had been broken once too often in training fights. He had the look of a top sergeant ready and able to take on half the men in his outfit at once. There was a gleaming intensity about the man that Mark saw and respected, but which he knew could also fuel the fires of revenge and indignation. As far as Mark could see, General Hemphill was not a man with much humor in his makeup.

If this were the general's usual Saturday night routine, he must be following it to the letter. So nothing was going to happen tonight, and Mark had no thoughts of jumping the general in his home; it would gain him nothing. Early tomorrow morning would be time enough to contact the general. Mark turned back to the BOQ and went inside. He lay on his bed and slept for four hours, waking promptly at four-thirty as he had commanded his mental alarm clock to rouse him. He was refreshed, alert, and ready for anything—totally recovered from his brush with sunstroke, even though the scratches remained.

Nothing had happened by 6:00 A.M. Mark was out on the base, driving around and testing the air.

By 7:00 A.M. there was a sudden burst of activity, and Mark saw the general arrive at his headquarters, dressed snappily in his uniform, carrying a short swagger stick as if it were a part of his arm. There was a grim smile on his face and that alone worried Mark.

At 7:30 A.M. Mark heard sirens go off around the base. He drove to a phone booth and called the operator.

"Sir, we are on an emergency class-one alert. This phone is for official use only. Is this an official call?"

"What is a class-one alert?"

"All personnel restricted to base, gates closed, all duty officers at their posts, standing by for potential attack. That's all I can tell you, sir." She cut the connection.

Mark was putting it together. A test alert, the commanding general could call such an alert to check on his security, to check a dozen different aspects of his base. And Sunday morning was an ideal time to do it. It would also be an ideal time to utilize the power he had as base commander. For the next few hours the base would be his kingdom, with no one he didn't want going in or coming out. He was all set, but now what the hell was he going to do?

When Mark left the phone booth he could see the base transform itself. The area was jumping with nervous energy. The class-one alert was not specified yet as to whether it was an actual attack or a test. Everyone on the base must be remembering what happened on another Sunday morning when the U.S. military was at weekend strength at certain bases and installations.

Mark got back in his rented car and drove around, heading for headquarters. The base was a jumble of activity: jeeps racing up and down the streets; AP's appearing at previously uncontrolled intersections directing traffic. The closer he came to the base HQ, the more activity he found. Fully half the uniformed men and women he saw now wore side arms or carried weapons.

Closer to the GHQ he found a perimeter of armed guards with M-16 rifles turning away all cars. He showed his ID to a sergeant who shook his head.

"Sorry, sir. No civilian traffic within the GHQ perimeter. With your ID you will be admitted on foot. That's the best we can do."

Mark parked the car and walked through the screen after showing his ID to three officers. They asked him why Justice, and he just smiled at them. He still had his own .45 safely in place in his belt holster.

At the door to the general's headquarters Mark found a dozen guards, all with automatic rifles. Yesterday there had been one lonely, bored Office of Security Investigations man with a pistol on his white belt.

Mark told his story three times before he was allowed inside the headquarters. He started with a sergeant and finished with a captain who looked nervous enough to run. Inside he was directed to a corporal who attached himself to Mark, asked where he wanted to go, and said he was the guide who would escort him there. The man led the way through a half dozen corridors and past several interior guards before they came to an outer office door with two armed guards.

Mark again showed his ID and they opened the door for him. Inside were a dozen men, all in uniform, sitting in chairs, watching the double doors opposite them. To the side was a desk occupied by a trim air force woman corporal.

"I'd like to see General Hemphill; it's most urgent," Mark said.

"The general is extremely busy this morning. As

you must know, we're on a class-one alert. I don't think he'll be able to see you for some time."

Mark showed her his Justice Department ID card and she lifted her brows. She took the card, made a Xerox copy of both sides and returned the original.

"Sir, I'll see that the general gets this with a note. I'm sure he'll want to talk with you."

Mark sat down. There were three colonels in the room, their eagles temporarily grounded; two majors; and the rest captains. All were cooling off, waiting for the big man. Mark decided he'd give the brigadier exactly fifteen minutes; then he was going to demand that he see the general at once.

At precisely 7:00 A.M., Pacific Standard Time, Air Force One experienced a total communications failure on board. A bent pin, two feet of bell wire, and a direct short from the plane's main electrical power cable was all it took. There would be nothing left of the vaporized safety pin or the bell wire and nothing to inplicate Sergeant Grout. He had his alibi all worked out. He was blown backward by the electrical explosion in the console. One panel after another shorted out, spurting smoke and flames for an instant, charring circuit boards, blasting apart diodes and transistors, and ruining nearly three hundred thousand dollars worth of intricate electronics gear. Sergeant Grout suffered first-degree burns as he smothered the small fires with a blanket.

Major Craig ran up before the last of the fires was out.

"What the hell happened, Grout?"

"She blew, sir. I was sitting here watching dials and she blew sky-high. Let me see what's still functioning."

He sat back down at the console, flipping switches, checking some of the smoke-smeared dials.

"Not much left, sir. I think we've still got CW, but I can't even get the pilot on the intercom."

"All right, Grout, see what you can patch together. We've got to land for repairs. I'll check with the navigator. Where the hell are we anyway?"

"I heard the pilot say something about being over China Lake a couple of minutes ago. Isn't that near Los Angeles?"

"China Lake. Yes, navy. And right next door to Edwards. We could set down at Edwards. I'll get back to you."

Major Craig ran through the compartment door toward the president's quarters. A moment later he was with the navigator, getting location confirmation. Two minutes later they called Edwards Air Force Base in California and were given permission to land.

"Air Force One, this is Edwards AFB. You're cleared for runway two-niner. Colonel, we are in the middle of a class-one alert, basewide. As a condition of that alert you are instructed to taxi to station 14, and on to building 751. General Hemphill sends his respects to the president and requests that if the president wishes to leave the plane while at Edwards, he is requested to follow the direction of the OSI to keep our alert procedures intact. It should cause no inconvenience to the president."

"Edwards, Air Force One acknowledges. Would there be a facility the president could utilize while on the ground?"

"Yes, Air Force One. The designated building 751 is set up for VIP transients, being recently renovated and upgraded. We believe it will serve the president well while he is here. There is seclusion, and tight security. There is also adequate space for the president's own security people to function inside the facility. Additional security can be placed around the compound if needed."

"Is communication available? We've had a problem with our on-board communication equipment and need landlines available for emergencies."

"Unfortunately, Colonel, there is at the current time a problem there. We are experiencing failures on all landlines we have, including those carrying commercial news and entertainment. We're not sure what is going on, but it seems to be some sort of protest or strike. We have sporadic communications by our own radio net, but evidentally the commercial lines between cities are out—almost one hundred percent around the nation."

"Thank you, tower. We're in the landing pattern. Will advise."

When the big Air Force One landed it taxied to the specified area. Two of the president's Secret Service men left the plane at once to inspect the facility. It was set back from the taxi strip five hundred feet and well away from the operational runway. There were eight buildings, and a quad with four more around them to provide a court. A barbed wire fence surrounded the entire compound and the perimeter was being patrolled by men with M-16 rifles.

Inside, the buildings were set up to meet the needs of a wide variety of people, and one structure was furnished with all the comforts the president could want. The security men returned and suggested that the president move temporarily into the new facility until repairs could be made on the radio equipment.

Twelve Secret Service men surrounded the president as he made the short walk down the ramp and across a short stretch of the tarmac to the gate of the VIP rest area. Then quickly inside the first building, through that and into the second building, and the Secret Service men relaxed a little, moving around and checking on every aspect of security

125

they could think of, at last concentrating on the inner core, allowing no one in the area without specific approval by the president or his senior staff members.

The president smiled as he stepped into a fully equipped office and sat down in a large leather swivel chair behind a massive cherry-wood desk. His smile faded into a look of concern.

"Gentlemen, find out at once what this communications blackout is all about, what it means. Captain Richardson, see if you can get any reading on the military. Have there been any threats or any attacks on our nation? Check this out as soon as you can—it's vital."

The captain nodded and left for the plane. However, that would do no good if the radios were out. He went into another room and picked up a base telephone.

The president tented his fingers and worried. He was hopelessly in the dark. At this very moment the DEW line could be sending a warning of enemy ICBM's arching toward major American cities. With no communications he wouldn't even know about it, perhaps not for days after they hit! He could not order a retaliatory strike. The navy had the most powerful radio network around the globe. He ordered a naval attaché to see if he could contact navy radio and get an assessment of the situation.

One of the Secret Service men put a Handie-Talkie type radio down near the president.

"Mr. President, this is our communication with the plane. I'll be here to send and receive any instructions you might have."

The president nodded.

"Does anyone know where Air Force Two is? It had identical communications gear with One, does it not?" Someone agreed with him. "Try and locate it and get it out here. Perhaps we could utilize it quicker than we could fix the radio gear."

An aide left for another telephone.

"Harvey, get on a base phone and keep in contact with the best radio operation this base has, and keep me informed of any news of importance that can be picked up. I especially want to hear of any attacks on our nation or possessions."

He watched the faces of the ten or twelve other friends, advisers, and political assets in the room with him. "Gentlemen, this is a serious situation. Someone knocked out our communications, and they must have had a reason. Let's all pray to the Lord Almighty that this reason is not predicated on an attack of our cities by hydrogen bombs. Now, let's settle down and try to figure out who did this to us, and what they hope to gain."

The fifteen minutes Mark had allowed were not quite up when an officer with major's leaves on his collar came through a door and went to the secretary. She pointed to Mark, who stood. The major motioned him forward and they went in the door he had left partly open. It was a side office.

"Colonel, we're in a bit of a hassle here right now. We had scheduled this practice alert for a month. Now we're in the middle of a national communications blackout, and to top it off the president of the United States just landed here in Air Force One after sustaining massive damage to the onboard radio communications system. He's safe and being well protected, but it all makes things unusually hectic.

"The general asked me if I might be able to help you. He wants to find out what Justice wants with us. What I'm doing is a screening to try and speed up his work load."

"I understand, Major, and I appreciate it. But frankly, my business comes from very high in the administration and is something I must discuss with General Hemphill himself. This must all be in the strictest of confidence. I know that doesn't make your job any easier, and I was going to say you could call Washington and check my credentials, but I'm afraid that's not possible now. You say there's a total blackout of landlines communications: radio, TV, telephone, telegraph, ticker tape, everything?"

"That's what we understand. Local telephone is no problem and local TV shows and radio. But they don't get any network news wire and no national or international news at all."

"Why, Major? Have we been attacked?"

"Nobody knows about it if we have. There have been no reports of attacks. Our air force radio network usually relies on lots of landlines, but now it's trying on one hundred percent pure air transmissions and we get only intermittent reports. But so far we have no word of any attack anywhere."

"Then something else is going on we don't know about. Have the unions made any demands? Who is going to gain anything from this blackout?"

"No one seems to know. The president is aware of the problem. We told him about our alert and he's cooperating. General Hemphill talked to the president about it; he understands the minimal restrictions it places on him, and he has agreed. We aren't bothering him but he's grounded until they get the radios working again anyway. It's all highly unusual."

Mark nodded. Wasn't it a coincidence that the president's plane arrived at the same time as the blackout and at the same time it had a total failure of on-plane commo gear? And strange that it was near the base where General Hemphill had bought himself a blackout. Even stranger that there was a first-class alert on the same base called by that same commander. Now, more than ever, Mark wanted to see General Hemphill and he couldn't afford to wait.

Chapter 10

AND NOW . . . THE PRESIDENT!

Mark watched the general's aide, who had just briefed him on the state of the emergency at Edwards Air Force Base and what they were trying to do about it.

"Major, it is vital that I talk with the general without delay. I've already been waiting fifteen minutes and valuable time is slipping away. My mission concerns the president and this current crisis. I think we'd better break in on the general no matter what he's doing. This is truly an emergency of national importance, Major, and the general is the one man who can show me how to help. Is there any insurmountable reason why we can't go see the general right away?"

"Colonel Brown, ordinarily I never do that. But as you say, these are strange times, and unprecedented." He looked at the intensity of Mark's stare and nodded. "Yes, let's go in the side door. Let me talk to the general for a moment."

131

They walked down a hall and stepped into an office nearly twenty feet square. At the far side a platform had been built eighteen inches above the rest of the room. On this level sat a large desk with General Hemphill planted firmly behind it. He looked down on everyone else in the room. At the moment the commander of the base was talking to a bird colonel who had a frown on his face a half meter wide.

The room was right out of the movie "Patton," with a huge U.S. flag on one wall, a dozen battalion flags on another showing the crests and banners from outfits the general had commanded in the past. A large golden eagle—not a fake—well preserved by taxidermy, soared over the desk on spread wings held aloft by thin wires.

A dozen chairs had been lined up to face the general's desk. The carpet seemed three inches deep to Mark as he stepped onto it. Framed color and black and white pictures covered one whole wall. The general looked up questioningly at the major.

"Sir, could I have a moment?"

General Hemphill scowled, held up his hand to the bird colonel he had been talking to and nodded. The major strode briskly to the desk and talked in low tones for a few sentences, then showed the general the copy of Mark's Justice Department ID.

General Hemphill took the ID at once, dismissed the two officers, and waited until they had left the room. Hemphill glanced at the ID again, then walked to where Mark stood. They were alone in the big office. He held out his hand.

"Well, well, this is a pleasure, a real live Justice Department agent. I've heard a lot about your good work. As you know, we're having a few problems here this morning. What can I do for you?"

"General Hemphill, do you know Victor Jerele from Phoenix?"

"Jerele? Is he a military man? Where did you say he was from?"

"General, don't bullshit me. You know him. I saw a muscle over your right eye tighten when I said the name. You know him; you hired him to create this nationwide communications blackout. Let's not spar around. I know you did it. What I want to know is why?"

Hemphill chuckled. "How could I do such a thing, you must be joking."

"It's no joke, General. Whatever small-stakes game you're playing could backfire on you. Don't you realize the vulnerable position you've shoved your country into? Think what an enemy could do right now if it wanted to. Russia could blow us off the map with ICBM's and we would have no way to order a retaliation. We might not even know for days some of the attacks that hit us!"

Hemphill laughed. "Yeah, that's the truth. We could be in one hell of a mess." He scowled and lifted a finger, shaking it at Mark. "Well, Buster, that is all just tough shit! That's what it is. But it isn't gonna happen. The Russians won't attack, 'cause they don't *know* the situation. After that it's a calculated risk and I took it. Yeah, I took it. I ordered the commo blackout, I even paid for it. And there won't be an attack. I'll give you my personal guarantee."

"General, your guarantee is more bullshit, and you know it."

The commander went over and sat behind his big desk.

"Son, I don't know why the hell you came here this morning, but if you've got any clout with Uncle Sam you better get on the horn and talk to whoever's left back there in Washington."

"Why? About the blackout?"

"Hell no. You don't know what's going on do

133

you? I had figured I'd have to use somebody else, but hell, I'll just go with you. You haven't got a glimmer of what this is all about, do you?"

"The blackout?"

"No, dumbass, about the president."

"The president? I know he's here."

"Damned right he's here. I brought him here and now he's under my total command. I just kidnapped the president of the United States. Neither he nor his group or his plane is going to leave this base until I say they can. He and his whole staff and crew are my prisoners."

Mark's heavy brows came half down over his eyes as he stared at the man. Ridiculous. Or was it? So many small coincidences started making more and more sense. They weren't chance happenings at all. What if they were all elements of a carefully orchestrated plan? It could be. Somehow this nut might have done it.

"I find that hard to believe, General," Mark said, stalling, furiously trying to figure some kind of plan, some defense, some offense, even an idea. He was staggered.

"It's true, Buddy Boy, damned true. Only one small factor that might surprise you. That cracker don't even *know* he's a prisoner. None of his people know it either. They think he's just waiting over there in our VIP place until his plane is ready, and they are delighted that we have such ready-made security for him. The president has better security by far than he would in the White House."

"Now you're bluffing me, General. I flat out don't believe you."

"Hell, don't trust me; I'll show you, give you a guided tour."

"I insist on it," Mark said.

The general went to Mark and held out his hand.

134

"I'll take your piece. I know you carry one."

"You think I'd start a one-man war against this army of yours?" Mark had bought the used .45 in LA before he left.

"I don't want to take that risk. Give me your piece or you don't get to say howdy to the president."

Mark handed the general his .45 by the barrel. The general took it and put it on his desk, then led Mark out the same side door they had come in.

Five minutes later and with both one-star flags flying on the front fenders, the general's car pulled up outside the barbed wire enclosure. Mark looked at it carefully. It began with a double-apron barbed wire combat fence on the bottom, then lifted into a ten-foot chain link fence with concertina on top and with guarded towers. It looked like a prison.

"Show me the perimeter," Mark said. The general smiled and ordered his driver to go around the facility, slowly.

Mark watched the plot plan unfold. The security was undeniable. The fencing, and OSI guards stationed every twenty-five feet, and all with helmets, M-16's, and extra bandoliers of ammunition. The area was about a block square, with a tennis court inside, a new-looking swimming pool with no one in it, several small service buildings, and one airman riding a self-propelled lawn mower working on the grass.

"As you'll notice, Colonel Brown. There is only one entrance, this tunnellike affair of barbed wire and concertina we're coming up to now."

Mark had counted at least eight good-sized buildings inside the fence arranged in roughly two quads, with the outer one built around the inner one.

"You put all this up especially to hold the president while you make him believe he's a guest?"

"Hell no. This was an old disciplinary barracks.

135

We simply renovated certain buildings and added the pool. It makes an ideal resting spot for VIP's. The former president used it quite often. It really was constructed for the convenience of high-ranking heads of state: kings, shahs, premiers, the like."

The general smiled, his beaming face on the verge of a huge unsupressed joke.

"But at the same time all the security can be quickly reversed to keep the president and his party inside the compound," Mark said.

"Precisely, Colonel. I'm glad you can see that. You're not the idiot some of those government people are."

They stopped at the barbed wire tunnel, and the general motioned to Mark. "Shall we take a quick guided tour inside? I'm sure we can see the president for a moment."

Mark nodded. The entrance was guarded by a barbed wire gate, and a crew of six armed men. The general was saluted at the gate but had to show two ID's to get past it. The tunnel itself was made entirely of concertina, roll upon roll of it stretched out over a framework of two-by-fours leaving an eight-foot tunnel. The whole thing was about fifty feet long and extended from the outer fence to what Mark now saw was an inner fence six feet high topped with concertina.

At the far end of the tunnel was another gate with more OSI guards both inside and outside. Again the ID was shown by the general and he was allowed to pass through.

Mark saw more guards moving around among the buildings. They walked past the first outer set of structures, then toward the inner court. Twice they were challenged, identified themselves, and allowed to pass. The general was right. Nobody was going to blast his way either in or out of this trap without a lot of firepower, and taking heavy losses. The

136

president had not more than fifteen armed Secret Service men with him. General Hemphill could throw four thousand men into the fight if he had to.

They passed an open stretch of grass and came to the inner core of the buildings. An OSI guard stood at the door of the first structure with his weapon. He saluted the general but remained firmly in front of the door, blocking the way.

"Sir, special authorization is required to enter this building."

"Yes, airman, I understand that. I'm Brigadier General Hemphill. Here is my ID card and special authorization badge. This other officer is an official of the government, a Justice Department agent I'm vouching for." The general held out a plastic case with his ID in it. Then he took Mark's ID and gave it to the guard. The airman looked at all critically, then handed them back to the general, came to a snappy present-arms salute with his rifle, and stepped aside. The general returned the salute and opened the door.

Inside, Mark found two more guards. They both saluted. The general returned the salutes with a half wave and walked to his right down a pleasant, carpeted corridor. At the second hallway he turned to the left. A civilian stood at the second door. Mark guessed he was a Secret Service agent.

"General Hemphill, sir. It's good to have you here. Would you like to see the president?"

"Yes, sir, I would. Thank you."

"Just a moment, sir. Let me check."

The civilian went through the door and they saw another man just inside.

"You'll notice, Colonel Brown, that our own OSI men guard the outer rings of this facility, and the inner rings. Only the last section where the president waits is controlled by the Secret Service. Does that tell you something?"

Mark was convinced. The crew could hold the president and his party inside this VIP prison for as long as they wanted to. All they had to do was turn around and point their weapons in the other direction.

Quickly Mark considered alternatives. He could wait until they got to the president, then challenge the general, reveal the plan to the president, and let happen what would. But could it work? Would the president believe him? He would have to gain their attention somehow, such as by grabbing the general and shouting at the Secret Service men.

The problem was that all too often such tactics anywhere around a president led to several bodies with holes in them. The Secret Service men would not hesitate to gun him down if they thought he was in any way threatening the Chief of State even in the slightest manner. No, he couldn't make any overt demonstration. Could he even mention the plot? The general would laugh it off, comment on the security the president had, and they both would leave and quickly be back in the area controlled by the AP where Mark would be quickly disposed of.

Mark sighed. It couldn't be a simple exchange of queen pieces on a chess board. He'd have to go along with the charade now and hope for a break later. He could always get back in if he needed to.

The Secret Service man came back smiling and ushered them into a modern office, not as big as the general's but at least sixteen feet square. The president sat at a desk, with a telephone in one hand. He said a few words into it, hung up, and stood.

"General Hemphill, sorry we had to crash in on you this way with no warning. But you have delightful quarters here for traveling gypsies, and the whole staff appreciates it. I wish to commend you and your people highly."

138

"Thank you, Mr. President. We hope that your stay here is pleasant. Sorry about the problems on board your aircraft. I can lend you equipment or men to help work on it if it would be of any assistance."

"Thank you, General. I believe that has already been done. Your Major Zedicher is doing well for us. Now, I'm afraid I better get back to work. General, I'm pleased you took the time to come by and see me."

"Sir, this is Colonel Brown, who is helping me this morning. I knew he'd want to meet you."

"Good morning, Colonel Brown, it's good to meet you."

"Thank you sir, the honor is mine," Mark said.

"Yes, thank you very much sir," General Hemphill said, giving the president a perfect West-Point-stiff salute, stepped back a pace, did an about-face and walked out of the room with Mark.

Once on the other side of the door and away from the Secret Service man, the general grinned, then laughed softly.

"You see how easy it is, Colonel? They are trapped but they don't even know it. A pity in a way that our president could be taken in so easily."

"Yes," Mark said, "a real shame. But the tragedy is that a general class officer would turn traitor and even think of trying to kidnap the president."

"Don't give me that shopworn patriot shit, Colonel. I just found out that my request for retirement has been accepted. You know why? I've given thirty-five years of my life to the service; now they are booting me out because I've been passed over twice for promotion. No second star, so out I go. A man has to maintain some pride. But pride is hard to eat. You think I want to suck up to some industrialist so I can get a big job that I don't know anything about just so he can use my name on defense

139

contracts? I belong in the air force. They should let me stay. Instead I plan on retiring at once, today, a shotgun retirement, and a life of luxury in some watering hole where the rich play. Oh, I'll move around, be impossible to find, and I'll enjoy myself for the rest of my life. A man can have a lot of fun with five million dollars, all tax-free."

"That's your asking price?"

"Yes, for now. If it can be done quickly. When we get back to my office I'll explain what I want, how to do it, and how you can contact Washington and relay my demands."

Ten minutes later they were in the general's office and he gave Mark the ultimatum.

"Colonel Brown, in a moment we'll go into my ham radio room. I've been a ham radio operator for years, and now it will function in a practical way. This is the procedure: I'll call Washington and make my contact. He will then find out whom you want him to reach. When he has your man patched through in his telephone, we talk. I'll give him the ultimatum, and he'll take it to the National Security Council, who will act. We'll talk in coded words, and my man will translate them on the other end. I'll want some voice identification from you, so your man will know that you're here and that everything I say is true and incontestable. Do you agree to co-operate or shall I shoot you right here and now?"

Mark had a trapped feeling he had never experienced before. There seemed to be no flaw in the design. There was nothing he could do yet to counter the move. He could kill the general, but would that stop the plan the bigwig had set in motion? This maniac had figured it out too well. Slowly Mark nodded in answer to the general's question. He could gain nothing by dying, not yet at least.

140

"Good, Brown. Let's get to it. My blackout can't hold out for more than two or three more hours. This must all be done and I must be on my jet before that. Hurry now!"

They went through another door and up a stairway to a sunny room with windows on three sides. On a bench was an expensive ham radio outfit, and on the wall dozens of CQ's from all over the country and some from Europe.

General Hemphill and Mark were alone. The general sat down and adjusted some knobs, turned on switches and went on the air.

It took him five minutes to raise the contact he was trying for in Washington. The voice transmissions came through remarkably clear.

"Yes, George in DC I read you loud and clear. This is Ginger Bear. I need a patch from you. Can you put me through to Dan Griggs in the Justice Department? I know this is Sunday but there's a chance he's there. Most urgent."

"Yes, Ginger Bear I read you here five-by-five. Will try your patch. Give me two minutes. Over."

The general looked at his watch and grinned at Mark. "Almost done, the fat is just about to jump into the fire. Watch it sizzle."

Soon the set came to life again as DC George was back on the air.

"Ginger Bear I have your party, Griggs in Justice, you're patched through, go ahead."

"Dan Griggs, this is Ginger Bear, your contact by phone there in Washington will translate everything for you. Write this down and listen carefully. I have a Colonel Brown here who is confirming my statements. Now take this down:

"The bird has come home to rest. All your eggs are in this one nest and it will require five million tries to get them out."

141

"That is the message. Your man here has ten seconds to identify himself."

Dan took the mike. "Dan this is Colonel Brown at Edwards AFB. Having some problems here. Best to follow directions."

The general's hand pulled away the mike.

"That's all, Griggs. You have two hours to reply and give me your specific directions."

The general signed off and turned off the set. He checked his watch. It was 8:15 on the coast, 11:15 in Washington.

"See how simple that was? Now we wait."

"It won't do you any good, Hemphill," Mark said.

"Oh, but I'm afraid you're wrong. They will have to pay; they simply have no choice. Everything has been planned, Colonel Brown. For the past year I have been plotting and figuring and planning this whole campaign. I was always good at tactics. Ever since they forced me into retirement I've been working on it. My plan is absolutely foolproof. Even an idiot can make it work now, and I assure you, I am not an idiot."

He knocked twice on the door and two men came in. One had handcuffs, the other an M-16 rifle aimed at Mark.

"These gentlemen will handcuff you and make sure you stay up here in the next room. Until you're needed again on the radio. You'll have to talk to your Mr. Griggs. Your performance was effective, a little stilted, but passable. And I like the way you slid Edwards in there, that will confirm the code words." The general frowned. "Men, better put leg irons on him as well. I don't like the easy way he moves, or the glint in his eye. He might be trouble."

"Yes, sir. As soon as we get him put in his room."

Hemphill watched Mark, his mouth heralding a
142

smile across his face. "Don't be so downhearted, Colonel. You don't know everything that was in the message. When the code is translated, your Mr. Griggs will discover that not only do I demand five million dollars in old one hundreds, but that if the cash is not delivered within an hour after the deadline here to the base by chopper, the bomb will go off. You see there is an extremely large charge of plastic explosive planted directly under the president's desk in the VIP area. That charge will be detonated at the end of the two hours. Don't look so surprised, Colonel. It's a small incentive to encourage the powers that be in Washington to get the money as quickly as they can and move it here. It can come from the Treasury Department's Los Angeles Federal Reserve District office.

"Also, your Mr. Griggs will be instructed that there is to be absolutely no attempt made to contact the president or his Secret Service men. If the president or his men hear about this from any source, the president will be blown up immediately.

"Don't look so sad, Colonel. Accept this as an accomplished fact. There is nothing you can do about it now, positively nothing."

Chapter 11

GOOD-BYE OLD FRIEND T-BIRD

Mark went with the two guards into the next room without an objection, then just before the closest one put the handcuffs on him, Mark slammed his flat hand against the guard's chest, checking his heart and dropping the man to the floor. Mark kicked the M-16 away from the other guard, smashed him to the floor, and used the handcuffs on him before he realized what had happened.

When Mark checked the first man, he saw that he had recovered; his heart was beating normally again, but the airman was still groggy. Mark tied his hands with some monofilament fishing line he always carried in his pocket, then put both men side by side and tied their legs together. They would have a hard time moving far. The general wouldn't be back in the radio room for at least an hour, maybe two; so it should be some time before Hemphill knew Mark had escaped.

Mark checked the room and saw a second door

that opened into a different stairway. This one probably would not come out in the general's office. At the bottom of the steps Mark cracked the door and peered out. He was in a short hallway that led to a door opening to the outside.

The Penetrator went through the door and then leaned against the outside of the building for a moment. A plan was starting to form—it was a little crude, but bold and just wild enough that it might work. It entailed some chances but that was all Mark had left. But before he did anything, anything, he had to take one more look at the VIP prison. How hard would it be to penetrate?

He couldn't get in with only his own ID. There was no time to wait for darkness. That left only the Wind Walker technique borrowed from the best of the Cherokee Dog Soldiers' medicine of a hundred years ago. Did he really need to get inside again before he tried the rescue? Yes. He didn't know the layout well enough. And he wanted to warn the president and get him away from that deadly desk. This trip really was necessary.

Mark got back into his car. Outside the guard perimeter where he had left it and drove as close as he could get to the VIP compound. He walked past two roving guards then a third asked to see his ID. He showed it to him and said he was working with the Secret Service on the president's security. The OSI sergeant let him past.

Now Mark moved in closer to the yawning mouth of the barbed wire tunnel gate. It was metal and had barbed wire layered over it. There was no way even for the Wind Walker to get past it unless it were opened. He'd wait for someone else to go through.

Mark stood to one side, as if waiting for someone. He checked his watch and looked around. He was about fifteen feet from the gate. One of the Secret Service men came, showed his ID and pass to the

146

guards who knew him from his frequent trips in and out, and the gate swung open wide.

Mark had been preparing his body and mind for the Wind Walker movements. He darted one way and then another, moving at an angle, and those watching saw only a flicker of movement, but never a person. Mark darted through the gate behind the Secret Service man, then ahead of him and then behind him. By that time the guards on the gate turned their backs to him, and he slowed his movements and fell into step a dozen paces behind the other man walking through the tunnel of barbed wire. There was no check on credentials at the other end of the tunnel.

Mark got there just as the other man was leaving, held up his hand, and the guard waited and let him through as well. The Penetrator walked toward the farthest building in the group with a sure, steady stride. He was inside now, and he had only the casual guards to worry about until he tried to get into the building where the president was staying.

Time! He had so little time. Mark didn't want to look at his watch. He came from the rear toward the building housing the president. There was one guard; no one else was in sight. Mark used the Wind Walker technique so the guard never knew for sure that anyone was coming. When Mark was behind the young AP guard, he made sure the door was unlocked; then he pushed the guard into the grass and darted inside the door before the startled air policeman could see him. Mark heard a yell from the other side of the door, but he walked normally down the hall remembering there would be more AP guards inside somewhere.

Mark had just come around a corner when a guard showed directly in front of him. The young man smiled and held out his hand to see Mark's pass. Mark gave him the Justice ID and the young airman smiled.

"Justice Department. Well, we don't see many of those. Now what about your special compound pass?"

Mark looked surprised, confused. "I came in with General Hemphill, he didn't say anything about any other pass." Mark looked down the hallway and saw civilian clothes. It was the same guard who had been at the president's door not forty-five minutes ago.

"Sir, I need a small favor here. Will you vouch for me?" Mark said.

The civilian looked blank for a moment, then nodded. "Yes, you are the Justice Department man who was here with General Hemphill earlier this morning. What's the matter?"

"He doesn't have the compound pass, sir," the airman said.

"That Justice Department agent ID is plenty good, airman. I'll vouch for this man. Thank you."

The airman saluted and walked away.

"Now, where were you heading? Did General Hemphill abandon you?"

"Yes, and I wanted to see the president again."

"Oh, that's a little unusual."

"True. The general is a ham radio nut, and he just got into touch with Washington through another ham. A telephone patch I think he called it. I have an urgent message from my chief in Justice, Dan Griggs. It's a message for the president. Can I see him?"

"He always is busy. Let me check that ID of yours again."

"Yes of course," Mark showed it to him.

"Colonel Brown. All right, let me check with him first."

They walked back down the hall to the door and

the man knocked, then opened it and vanished. He returned in less than a minute.

"The president is interested in any communications from Washington. He asks you to come right in."

The president was sitting at his desk, but stood when Mark came in. A second agent across the room was standing as well and watched Mark. He frowned and came over.

"Sir, I'll have to ask for your personal weapon while you're with the President."

Mark showed the empty holster. "General Hemphill already thought of that. He took my piece."

The agent went back to his chair and the president walked around his desk.

"Now, Colonel, what's this about some radio communications?"

Mark had to decide quickly just how much to tell the president. In an instant he decided to tell him everything.

"Mr. President, you may have trouble believing what I'm about to say, but bear with me. Your life and those of many of your people here may be at stake. The problem in your plane early today was sabotage, not an accident. Someone deliberately shorted out and blew up the communications systems so the plane would be forced to land at the nearest field, this one.

"The communications blackout across the nation was also engineered and paid for to happen at precisely the time your plane would land."

The president's eyelids lowered, his face set in a grim expression. "I had pondered that, and wondered about this facility that's so safe, so secure, and was here waiting for us."

"It's all a part of the plan, Mr. President." Mark had been speaking low so the other man in the big room could not hear. "This secure fortress you're in works two ways. The exterior rings of defense consist only of air force people. On orders, they can reverse their stance and prevent anyone from *leaving* this compound. The whole thing is a plot to kidnap you without your even knowing it, and to ransom you for five million dollars. It can work only if you and your people think all this security is for your protection and not designed to keep you here. If you tried to leave now you would be detained and there could be some shooting. With the nationwide news and communications blackout, there'd be no way for anyone to warn you or reach your plane. You're cut off from Washington, where the ransom message has been delivered."

The President's face showed more worry lines and now he went back to his desk and sat down. Mark shook his head and motioned the president away from the desk.

"I'm told there is a large bomb planted under the desk, sir. It can be set off at any time. It might be better if we went to another part of your quarters."

The president nodded.

"I'd suggest we move there at once; then I'll tell you the rest of the plot."

The president sighed. "My chief security man told me about the coincidences you mentioned. He was surprised also by the intricate security here. Then he found out it once was a prison. I think I believe you, Colonel Brown. I'm not too sure why, but I trust my instincts in these matters. And you and Tyson are thinking along the same lines."

"Let's go to your other quarters then, sir. That bomb still worries me. Exclude everyone you can from this building. All your staff. Then get one man you know and can trust, perhaps your chief of security. Get him to meet me so we can talk. I have a plan to get you out of here so even your own people won't know it. Would you show me where your other quarters are?"

The president beckoned to the Secret Service man. "Wilson, I'm going to my bedroom. Would you ask Tyson to come see me there? It's an urgent problem. I'd like to see him as soon as he can get there, please."

"Yes, sir, Mr. President." Wilson left the room practically running.

They went through another door, down a hall about a hundred feet into another room. This one was smaller, also without windows. Mark didn't like it. He checked the walls, the furniture. It must be bugged somehow.

A knock came almost at once at the door. Mark touched his fingers to his lips and the three men went into the hall.

"Find us another room, one nearby," Mark whispered. "I think this one is bugged."

They went on down the corridor into another room, and closed the door.

"This one is mine, Mr. President," Tyson said. "Who is this man?"

The president smiled. "Forgive me, gentlemen. Mr. Art Tyson, my chief of security, this is Colonel Brown, with the Justice Department security. I have a few things to tell you, Tyson. Your fears about the coincidences around here are evidently well founded. First, let's ask Colonel Brown if there is a time element?"

"Yes, sir. A little over half an hour ago, General Hemphill sent a message to Dan Griggs at Justice. It was a coded message demanding five million dollars ransom for you, Mr. President, and setting a two-hour time limit."

Tyson scowled and touched his weapon through his coat.

"Ransom . . . ?"

"I'll tell you later, Art," the president said.

Tyson was thinking. "It's obvious we can't fight our way out of this trap. If only . . ."

Mark continued, "I would suggest first, Tyson, you casually get as many people out of this building as possible. There's a bomb under the desk where the president was, in that office. Hold a briefing or something to pull all of your people out of here. Then, Mr. Tyson, I'd like you to meet me at the front gate in about a half hour. Oh, I'll need one of those special passes to get back in as well."

"You got in here without one?" Tyson asked, amazed.

"I'm sneaky sometimes," Mark said.

"But we have ironbound security, all those AP's . . ."

"True. Mr. Tyson, let's leave the president here in your room for now while we walk to the gate. I have some requests." On the way Mark gave Tyson the rest of his information about the ransom try. "Tell nobody else about any of this. Not even your most trusted lieutenant. Do everything yourself. To make this work we have to make General Hemphill think he still has the president. You'll be with the president at all times, and I'll fade out of the picture as soon as I'm sure he's safe. If your own men think the president is still in the compound, we might pull it off. Tell your men he's here, but he's taking a four-hour nap. Doctor's orders. Next get the items I write down on this list, and do what I suggest. Make it look like a good first-aid job."

They were at the tunnel. Tyson gave Mark one of the plastic passes and then took Mark's hand.

"Hell, this is against all my training, everything I've tried to do to keep the president safe. But I'll be damned if I don't think it's the only thing we can do now. Maniacs, the goddamned maniacs." He shook his head. "Okay, Brown, I'll get it all done, and meet you back here in twenty-five minutes. I just hope to God that it works." He turned and walked rapidly away.

It took Mark only a few moments to get through the two gates and outside, then he ran to his car. The plan had formed and solidified now. He checked in the trunk of the car and took out the two white-phosphorous grenades. He was trying to figure what the target should be. A five-million-dollar airplane was a cheap price to pay for a live president. Maybe he should find something cheaper. He drove toward the flight line and got as close as he could before AP's waved him off. He parked, dumped everything out of his aluminum case and put the two WP grenades inside. He showed his pass three times on his way into the smallest hangar at the end of the flight line. Inside he found only one forlorn T-Bird, the plane that taught thousands of men to fly jets for the first time—a workhorse and a favorite of many early jet flyers because it was so forgiving of pilot error. Mark walked around it once, then fastened the two WP grenades under the wing fuel tanks on one side and taped a two-minute timer-detonator to them. He activated the timer and walked away, still carrying the aluminum suitcase. Mark dumped the case at the hangar door, then walked slowly across the blacktop and had just cleared the AP's when he heard the explosion behind him. He turned and saw the smoke and flames, then went on to his car and drove to the closest phone booth.

Mark was nearly screaming into the phone when the operator came on at the hospital.

"Get some ambulances up the flight line. We've got a hangar on fire and explosions. Send four or five, and send one more ambulance to B-29 Avenue and Sixth. Right now, I've got a seriously injured man in a car wreck there. Rush it, we've got casualties!"

He hung up and went out to the street to wait. He heard sirens then, at least half a dozen, as ambulances rushed toward the flight line.

It took the ambulance three minutes to get to the street corner at Sixth. Mark waved them down and jumped into the front seat, pushing the rider over.

"The other guys got this accident victim. We need to go to the VIP compound. I'm Colonel Brown, M.D. I've got a seriously ill patient in the VIP compound. One of the president's men, I think. See how fast you can get there and use your sirens!"

The young airman driver gulped and jolted the ambulance into gear, ground around the first corner and shot down the street toward the VIP areas, his siren wailing.

He screeched up to the tunnel. Mark told him to back up to the gate and open the rear door. The three of them took the gurney out of the ambulance and Mark flashed his credentials and the pass as he screamed at them to open the gate. Then the men went through, running with the gurney inside the barbed wire tunnel. At the inner gate they found Tyson, who had the barrier open and now ran ahead of them leading the way.

They went down some steps, around four or five corners, then into the president's building. They hurried along a corridor and came to a door that Tyson unlocked. The latter winked at Mark, then pushed the door open.

"This is him," Mark said. "Get him on the stretcher. Don't bother checking him here, let's transport him stat. Come on, move him. I'm a doctor, for Christ's sake; I know what I'm doing. Move him."

The patient lay on the bed, one leg splinted, his face wrapped with gauze and tape so he couldn't be identified. One hand was wrapped as well. He was moaning.

154

They moved the president onto the gurney, strapped him down, and rolled the wheeled stretcher down the halls out to the sidewalk then to the barbed wire tunnel. Tyson was at the head of the procession. He yelled at them to get the gates open; then they were through and the medics lifted the gurney into the ambulance and folded the legs. They locked it in place.

Mark and Tyson jumped into the back of the ambulance and slammed the door. The ambulance sped away.

Mark moved to the front and yelled at the driver. "Don't take him to the base hospital. He's too critical; we've got to get him to the UCLA medical center. It's our only hope to save him."

"Sir, then he should go by chopper, much quicker that way," the driver said.

"No, we go by your ambulance," Mark countered.

"But sir, the chopper can get him there in thirty minutes. It'd take us three hours at least to drive."

"Head for Los Angeles," Mark barked.

"We don't have authorization to leave the base," the other medic said.

Mark nodded at Tyson to take out his piece. Tyson did so, moved up behind the driver, and put the .38 special muzzle behind the airman's ear. He showed him the end of the barrel, then put it firmly against the driver's head.

"Is that authorization enough?" Mark asked.

"Yes sir! Yes. What in hell is going on?"

Chapter 12

PRESIDENTIAL FOOTBALL MOVIE

Mark watched the two airmen closely as the ambulance wound along the Edwards Air Force Base road toward the gate.

"Do either of you men have loaded weapons?" Mark asked.

Both shook their heads.

"Look, this is nothing to get all shook up about, so don't do anything foolish. We're legitimate. The man back here with the gun is the chief security agent for the president of the United States. Now that's pretty high-ranking, wouldn't you say? He's got one of his men who must get out of the VIP compound and off the base, and this is the best way to do it. You men have had this ambulance off-base before, right?"

"Right," the driver said. "But we had transit papers for it and a real patient. I stop, give the papers to the guard, and he takes a copy and we go through."

157

"We can't do that today, so we fake it," Mark said.

"Sure, fake it, only how?" asked the driver.

"Pull up and don't quite stop, creep along slowly. Scream at the guard you've got a badly burned patient and no time to get transit papers. You've got to get him to the Palmdale Hospital, stat. Tell the guard the paper work is coming behind in a jeep. At that point if he doesn't let us go through, I'll lean out the back and start chewing tail. That should do it."

The driver looked at Mark quickly. "It sure as hell better, the gate is just up ahead."

The ambulance slowed, almost stopped at the AP guard. The guard yelled.

"Big fire on the base," the driver shouted. "They didn't give me any paper. We've got burn victims coming out our ass up there! Got to get this one into town fast. Paper work will come later in a jeep. Sorry, I got to move."

"Hold it!" the voice commanded from outside.

"What the hell's the matter out here? Sergeant, stand back, this patient is critical—unless you want to sign as the responsible party for his death!"

The guard turned and looked at Mark who had his full scowl on. The young sergeant gulped and shook his head.

"Move it, driver!" Mark shouted. "I've got to get back to my patient."

The guard reluctantly waved them through.

Once past the gate the three men in the rear of the ambulance cheered. They drove through Rosamond. Mark decided they would go on to Lancaster to be safer. They kept to the old highway road and headed the ten miles to Lancaster.

A short way farther on, Mark leaned over the front seat and quietly explained to the two medics what was happening.

"Men, in the back here you have a very special passenger. He's your boss really. Your passenger and former patient is the president of the United States, with a lot of gauze and tape on him. He's not ill or hurt. You're involved in helping to foil a complicated plot right here in the VIP facility to kidnap the president and hold him for ransom. That's a hard place to get inside, right. But it's twice as hard to get out of if someone wants to keep you there.

"That's about all you need to know right now. We'll find a motel in Lancaster for you, the president, and Mr. Tyson. You'll all stay there until this is over. Don't worry about being AWOL, we'll take care of that for you."

"You're joking, right?" the passenger-side medic said. "Joking about the president?"

"Pull over on the shoulder and stop the rig," Mark said.

A moment later when the ambulance had stopped, the president of the United States leaned into the front seat with all teeth shining and shook hands with both medics.

"I truly appreciate what you young men have done for me today," the president said. "And you can be sure that there will be an appropriate medal and commendation and promotion coming your way. I really mean that."

When the president went back to sit on the cot, Mark asked the young medic if he could still drive.

"Oh, damned right! Now that I know what's going on, and who is back there, I could drive you to hell and back! This is the greatest day of my life."

Fifteen minutes later they had rented a pair of motel rooms with connecting doors. The two airmen understood they were not to leave the room. They were still in awe of the president, even after he went into their room and sat on the bed and talked with them for several minutes.

159

Then Tyson called to the president.

"Mr. President, I know we didn't have time to bring any of the papers you were working on. But we do have something else to keep you busy. The local Los Angeles TV station has on a good football movie, *North Dallas Forty*."

The president grinned. "Men, how would you like to be my special guests at a movie? I'll even buy the peanuts?"

The men laughed and trooped into the president's room where the TV set was already on.

Mark motioned to Tyson.

"I'm going to get back to the base and talk Hemphill out of doing anything more rash than he already has, and try to wrap him up for the authorities. I've got your phone number here, and I'll give you the word just as soon as everything is cleared up at the base."

Tyson smiled. "Take your time. This is good for the president. No worry, no campaigning, no strain. I haven't seen him so relaxed in days."

"You'll hear from me."

Mark got into the ambulance, which was parked at the curb. He grinned, thinking how he had to pay for the motel rooms, since neither the president nor Tyson had any money. They seldom needed money on their official trips. But this one was certainly unofficial. The motel owner didn't even know who his patient-customer was. The only name on the register was Walter Tyson and party.

Mark wheeled the big ambulance into the street and made a U-turn, and twenty minutes later he had swung into the gate at the base. The guard had changed, and the man on duty at the in-coming side simply lifted his hand in a wave-on as Mark drove inside. Mark cruised toward the VIP compound, stopped three blocks short of it, and walked to where he had left his rented car.

From the jumble of weapons in the trunk where he had emptied out his case, Mark picked up the spare Ava, loaded it with sleep darts, and then drove back to the general's headquarters.

The security was less stringent now. Everyone knew it was only a test alert. Mark was given a cursory check with his ID as he went into the building and found the general's office. The corporal secretary was polite but firm. No one could see the general. Mark thanked her, and walked quickly through the door into the major's office where he had been taken before. He closed the door and snapped the lock before the surprised secretary could come after him.

The Penetrator went through the empty room into the hall and down to the back door of the general's office. Mark opened the door and stepped inside. General Hemphill was talking on the phone.

"Yes, have it on the flight line, warmed up and ready to go at eleven o'clock. Right." He hung up.

"Good morning, General. A beautiful day out today, isn't it?"

Hemphill turned and a roar bellowed from his throat.

"How the hell did you get away? Where have you been? We've been looking for you." The general came up with what looked like Mark's own .45 from the desk and aimed it at Mark.

"Yes, I can use it, don't make that mistake. Come on upstairs; it's time to call Washington again. Last time they hadn't done anything. It's time to call again."

Mark went up the steps to the radio room. The door to the other room was closed, and Mark didn't know if the two guards were still there or not. The general kept the gun on Mark as he flipped on switches, turned dials, and let the vacuum tubes warm up in his older-type ham set. He called Washington and got his contact on the first transmission. The reception wasn't quite as clear this time, but it was still good.

"George in D.C., we've had no word from you. What is the status of our project?"

"Still talking, Ginger Bear. I have Griggs on the horn and patched in. He wants to talk with Colonel Brown first.

"Government red tape, General," Mark said. "You know how that can be. I better talk to Griggs."

The general sighed and handed Mark the mike.

"Dan, are you there, buddy?"

"Colonel Brown. Griggs here. We've hit a snag."

"Don't worry about it. The man is safe and off the base. Cancel all talk about the five million, and don't worry about sending a fleet of SAC bombers over Edwards. The situation should defuse itself here within an hour. Repeat, the man is safe and off the base."

"Yes, Brown, read you. That's a relief, to say the least. My congratulations. I owe you one."

"No, Griggs, that makes at least six or seven you owe *me*. Oh, Ginger Bear here is about to pop. He wants some air time, I think."

General Hemphill grabbed the mike. "Griggs, when do you give me an answer? Disregard anything Brown said; he hasn't done a thing. You only have a little under half an hour to come up with a plan to get the money to me. Then I push the button and it's good-bye everyone. I'll blow him to hell and not twitch an eyelash. You remember that and get back to me."

He signed off and turned off the equipment. Then General Hemphill turned to Mark, the .45 still in his hand and aimed at Mark.

"Now, you slippery son of a bitch, talk. What in the hell did you mean the president is safe and off

162

the base? I checked not five minutes ago with the president's own security people and they said he was getting a little itchy, but he knew he had to wait for the plane to get back into operation. Everything is status quo at the VIP compound. My people say so as well. So the president is still there."

"I'll give you two-to-one odds on that, General. Like to take a thousand-dollar side bet. You better check again. I don't think any of your security people will be able to find him. Oh, you might also ask them if an ambulance called at the compound to take out a seriously ill person. Heart attack I think it was."

The general's eyes bulged for a moment, then his face turned red and he jabbed his hand at a telephone. His call went through to the security office at the compound.

"General Hemphill here, Captain. Did an ambulance come there recently and take someone out?" He paused and listened. "It did. And you didn't check to see who was under those bandages?" There was a pause. "No one checked. The doctor said it was an emergency. I'll bet it was! Contact the president's top security man, and tell him you have a message from me that must be delivered personally. Then simply demand to see the president in person at once. You have five minutes. If for any reason anything goes wrong, call me."

He hung up, and motioned Mark to go downstairs. The gun was still in his hand.

"Now, we will call your bluff, Colonel Brown. If it *was* the president you took out of the compound, I'll know in five minutes. If it's true, you die instead of him. Not a very big swap for me, but it will be all I'll have left, won't it?"

In the general's big office they waited. Major Zedicher came in and offered the general some papers,

163

but was waved out. He seemed surprised to see Mark there.

They waited, not talking. The phone jangled less than two minutes later.

"General, you can relax. I talked to the Secret Service man, the second in command for presidential security. He told me the president is well and happy and at the moment sleeping. He went into his bedroom about an hour ago with strict instructions not to be disturbed. So everything seems to be normal here. The president definitely is in the complex."

General Hemphill began to swear into the phone. "You stupid bastard! That's a screen. I'm coming over there right now. Don't do a damn thing until I get there. I don't even care if you breathe."

Mark was standing and moving toward the door before the general waved his weapon.

"Yeah, I know, move and don't breathe. You're a hard man to convince, General."

They arrived at the compound a few minutes later, and Mark got out and walked in front of the fence. He showed his own ID and pass, and the general stalked along behind.

Once through the barbed wire tunnel, they were met by a chubby captain who saluted smartly. General Hemphill had all he could do to keep from hitting the officer.

"Where is he supposed to be sleeping? Show me right now!"

The captain was shaking so much he could hardly walk. He led the way past guards and sentries and into the central core building. The captain went down the corridors until he came to two Secret Service agents.

The general still carried Mark's .45 in his hand. The agent looked at the general and stiffened.

"General, sir. That weapon must be put away. If

164

you persist in holding it, I'll have no alternative but to draw my own weapon and kill you. Do you understand?"

The general narrowed his eyes, shook his head slightly, and muttered something as he stuffed the .45 in his belt.

"Yes, yes. Sorry, I'm upset. I heard someone had kidnapped the president. I must see him at once; it's vital."

"This is highly unusual, sir. We're in complete charge at this level. You have no authority here. This man is your commander in chief."

"Exactly. If he isn't here and I've fucked up and let someone kidnap him right out from under my own security complex, I might as well cut off my head."

The Secret Service man sighed. "I appreciate your position, General. I don't see that it would hurt to let you look in on the president. First, I'll need to take your weapon."

General Hemphill handed it to the agent and they walked down the hall to the second door. It was Tyson's room. Mark grinned.

The Secret Service man unlocked the door and looked in; then he jolted inside and looked around. Hemphill dashed into the room behind him.

"He isn't here, you idiot! Is this the right room? Nobody's here!"

The frantic Secret Service man ran from the room, down to the president's original sleeping quarters and threw open the door. That space also was empty. He ran to the office and found no one behind the big desk. Slowly he took out his radio and asked for a report where the president was. No one had any information except that he was sleeping in Tyson's living quarters.

Mark went to the Secret Service man.

"Tyson says not to worry. He's with the president

off the base at a safe location. We have a problem to clear up here, and then the president will be back." The Secret Service man blinked.

"Who are you?"

"Brown, with the Justice Department. I went with Tyson—it's for the president's own safety. Believe me, he's safe. The general is the one we have to watch."

"Why should I believe *you?*"

"Remember the ambulance that came a short time ago?"

"Yes?"

"Who led the charge through the wire with the casualty?"

"Tyson."

"Who do you think was on that stretcher?"

Slowly the Secret Service man began to grin, then he laughed.

Mark looked up in time to see General Hemphill charging at him with absolute fury in his eyes. Mark sidestepped and tripped the general. The man fell heavily and rolled. When he came up it was like a pro football player getting up from one block and charging for another try at the ball carrier. In one hand he had two quarter-pound blocks of C-4 explosive.

"He's here somewhere. You're hiding him. But you can't get away with it. I'll blow us all up, and him with us. If I get this over there to the desk I can trigger the big bomb underneath."

Mark whispered to the Secret Service man. "There is a bomb here, evacuate all your personnel at once. Get them outside the barbed wire if possible. Move it now!"

The man took out his radio and was speaking into it as he ran out the door of the office into the hall.

Mark tackled the general before he got to the big desk. They rolled on the floor, but Hemphill was up

166

again like a rookie in spring training trying to make the team, and charged for the desk. Mark had seen the timer on the explosive package. The timer-detonator was real. The general could set off the deadly charge. Mark wasn't positive there was another bomb under the desk, but if there were the sympathetic explosion would set it off as well.

But there was no time to find out. Hemphill had crawled under the desk, and Mark ran for the office door. He was in the hall going away from the area when a blast shook the building. One wall came crashing in on him, and for a moment Mark thought he had run his last race. Then the wall sheared and most of it blasted over him, but he couldn't avoid all of it, and before he knew what happened, he felt something hit the side of his head and he went down. The floor came up hard, smashing against his body and hurting him all over before the power of the exploding bomb shattered his vision and his thought and he collapsed into darkness.

EPILOGUE

Mark woke up screaming. Someone was trying to rip his leg off his body. Dust filled his nose and when he tried to spit the chalky whiteness from his mouth, he gagged.

"Easy there, take it easy. You'll be all right."

Mark screamed again but felt his leg come free from something devastatingly heavy, and his eyes cleared as he looked up and saw a lovely smile below concerned blue eyes. She smiled again and then the blackness came down and he slumped on the stretcher.

When Mark came back to consciousness, the first thing he noticed was the coolness of his skin, then the brightness, and at last the hospital room. Then he saw the same concerned blue eyes and that wonderful smile and he remembered from the time of the pain and the explosion.

"Hi, sleepyhead. You had a long nap," the blue eyes said.

He blinked, shivered, and looked down from the blue eyes and saw that she was a beautifully formed, real-live girl. He swallowed, not sure if he could talk. His mouth still tasted of plaster dust. Then he thought of the time.

"What time is it?" he asked, his voice a croak at first, but coming up almost to normal at the end.

"It's four-thirty—sixteen-thirty—and this is still Sunday, August tenth, and you had a nasty hit on your head. How are you feeling?"

"Lousy." Slowly the time factor came through. "Four-thirty? I've got to make a phone call."

"If you're worried about Mr. Tyson, he called two hours ago. He says to rest, he's got everything under control." She watched him relax. "Now, are you hungry? You missed lunch."

Mark shook his head.

"First you want a rundown on the damage to your body, right?"

Mark nodded, grimly. He wasn't sure he could feel his right leg, his head pounded and he ached all over.

"Can you take the hard, cold facts, Colonel?"

"Yes, yes, go ahead."

"Good, patient shows a little spirit. First, your right leg. It isn't broken but nobody knows why. A cement wall was trying to break it. You got off with a deep gouge, a bone bruise and some stretched tendons. Also you have an extremely hard head." She grinned and he had to grin back at her. She had a delightful smile.

"Fine. Patient shows some sense of humor. Colonel, there is nothing to be worried about. From everything I've heard you're a hero. Oh, the rest of your injuries. You have a mild concussion and shouldn't do any running around for a while. The doctor says two days of bed rest should fix you up on the head. Outside of ten or fifteen bad cuts,

170

scratches, and scrapes, and a few beautiful black-and-blue marks, you're as good as new."

"Two days?"

She laughed. "I win. I made a bet with the doctor that's the first thing you would say when I told you. Now, one more test. What's five times twelve and a half?"

"Sixty two and a half, why?"

"I just wanted to make sure you have all the wires plugged in. When I think you're rational, I'm supposed to make a phone call for you. Do you feel like talking?" He nodded. She dialed a number she read from a piece of paper and gave the phone to Mark.

"Hello, Tyson here," a voice answered.

"Tyson. This is Colonel Brown. The nurse just dialed for me. What happened after I left?"

"You're the one I wanted to ask that. After I didn't hear from you for an hour, I phoned the base and found out all hell had broken loose. There was a massive explosion in the VIP compound; the general was killed as were two AP guards, and you got all mashed up. Colonel Franklin, the second in command at the base took over and ended the alert and got things back to normal. The guards were all off the VIP compound now and they're closing it. What the hell happened in there?"

Mark told him quickly, and simply explained that the general went crazy and tried to blow up the compound, hoping he could take the president along with him.

"Hemphill was mentally ill, there's no question of that. Oh, Air Force Two flew in about an hour ago. It's the duplicate of Air Force One and is all set to go. It was called in as soon as the technicians saw that the communications on-board One couldn't be repaired in time. So now the president is back on board and we're getting ready to continue his junket." He paused. "Are you getting too tired? Can you talk a little more?"

"I can talk all day. When you heard the base was secure, what did you do?"

"I called a taxi and we rode back to the field. When we got here I was embarrassed because, between the president and me, we didn't have enough cash to pay the cab fare. The medics came up with the money. The president was so abashed he told me never to be without a hundred dollars in my pocket after this." He paused. "Oh, Colonel Brown, there's someone here who wants to talk to you."

"Right."

The next voice on the wire was soft and slightly southern. Mark recognized it at once.

"Colonel Brown, I don't know how I'll ever be able to thank you for what you did today. If it hadn't been for you and your quick thinking and quick action, we might have a new president at this moment. Now, you don't need to say a thing, Colonel. I've got the whole story, or at least most of it. I've also talked to Mr. Dan Griggs in Washington and he's told me a little more of your interesting situation, a kind of part-time specialist for the Justice Department."

"It's always interesting working with Mr. Griggs and his people."

"We're going to make some changes in the laws of this land, Colonel Brown, you can be sure of that. We'll soon send to Congress legislation prohibiting any national unions in the communications field which could be used to black out sending and receiving again. We also will scatter key transmission facilities, making it much harder to knock out those microwave relay stations. And we will maintain a twenty-four hour radio network with all vital defense and armed forces facilities. We've grown a bit too complacent about our national defense communications. This little exercise has shown us how a tragedy could occur. So you see, some good has come from all of this after all."

"That makes me feel a lot better, sir. I'm still angry about the deaths of those two young AP's who died so needlessly."

"That wasn't your fault, Colonel. I'm impressed with your concern, but please don't burden yourself about it. Now, could I speak with your nurse for a moment?"

"Yes sir." Mark handed the phone to the nurse. "He wants to talk to you."

Mark watched as she took the phone.

"Yes. This is Lieutenant Johnson, RN."

Mark watched her face as blue eyes widened in surprise; then her mouth opened in wonder. She stammered a reply.

"Oh, oh, oh, yes, Mr. President. Colonel Brown is resting comfortably. He's not seriously wounded and should be up and out of here in two or three days."

She listened, her eyes still wide in astonishment as she looked down at Mark, who laughed soundlessly.

"Yes, yes, of course, Mr. President. I'll do my very best to take care of him. I most certainly will." She handed the phone back to Mark, the shock of speaking with the president still showing on her face.

"Yes, Mr. President," Mark said.

"Colonel Brown, I was wondering, would you do me a favor? I understand you are now only a part-time consultant and operative with the department. The government needs good men. There's always a place in Justice for you on a full-time basis. I'm sure that I can convince Dan Griggs that he needs you. We can make a considerable increase in the compensation you have been receiving."

"I'm sorry, Mr. President, that wouldn't be possi-

that he would be immensely proud to give it to you."

"Thank you, Colonel Brown, I'd appreciate that."

Mark said good-bye and hung up the phone. He reached and caught the nurse's hand. "How did you like talking with the president of the United States, your commander in chief?" She simply stared at him vaguely. "Lieutenant Johnson?" His voice took on a command tone and she blinked and looked down at him.

She sat on the chair beside his bed and leaned over.

"Do you know that I just talked with the president of the United States? Me, Lieutenant Johnson, talked to the president!"

He still held her hand.

"Yes, Lieutenant Johnson, I was aware of that. And what did he tell you to do?"

She frowned, then jumped up, and became super businesslike. "He said to take the best possible care of you, and not to let a single bad thing happen, and I told him I would. How is your leg? Does your head hurt? Do you need any pain medication? Is the TV set big enough? How would you like our projection screen model? Is there anything else I can do?"

Mark laughed at her sudden concern. He motioned her toward him. "There is one thing you can do. Lean down here." When she came close he put his good hand behind her neck and pulled her mouth the last inch to his and kissed her. Surprise on her lips turned to duty and then to pleasure and she moved away from him slowly.

"Oh, my goodness. Did the president mean I should kiss you that way too?"

"Exactly like that, Lieutenant Johnson. Now, you mentioned something about lunch a while ago. I'd like a two-pound steak, rare, just braise it on each side and leave it raw in the middle. A quart of orange juice and a quart of raw milk. If I'm sleeping when you come back, wake me up."

"Yes sir. Yes sir, Colonel sir." Then she bent and kissed him quickly again, murmured something deep in her throat, and hurried from the room.

Mark tried a deep breath and a sigh. Nothing hurt inside at least. He smiled remembering the surprise on Nurse Johnson's face when she realized she was talking to the president.

He looked around at the private room, the color TV set, the flowers, and a window that opened onto a wide green lawn. This might not be such a bad place to rest up for a couple of days, or three. He'd insist that Lieutenant Johnson be assigned to him full time. Without thinking about the news blackout he switched on a small radio beside the bed.

". . . and said there was a minimum loss of life because of the blackout. Our network reports that at this hour the entire nation is back in business, the landlines have been opened and with them the network TV and news wires and the radio networks as well. It looks like the big blackout is over and we can settle back to business as usual. Authorities in Washington still have made no comment on rumors that the blackout was part of a plot to kidnap the president. The president's party was in California at the time of the blackout and the president rested at the Edwards Air Force Base and test facilities just east of Los Angeles. Repairs were being made to the Air Force One's communications system at the same time.

"However a taxi driver in Lancaster, near the base, swears that he drove the president, two air force medics and a civilian from Lancaster the ten miles to Edwards just after noon today. Our own reporters are now investigating.

"In other news, just off a now-functioning

teletype: There has been a bad volcanic eruption in Greece. Authorities there say that . . ."

Mark switched off the radio. He did feel drowsy. Probably from some shots they had given him.

Later, when Lieutenant Johnson came in, he opened his eyes and watched her. He liked the way her uniform tightened and stretched as she moved. Delightful.

"Your lunch will be ready in twenty minutes, Colonel Brown," she said. "One steak dinner, rare, coming up."

He nodded, motioned for her to sit down, and held her hand as his eyes closed again. He could still see her blue eyes, her soft smile, and he knew that three days of rest here would not be hard to take at all. He still held her hand, and in his sleep the Penetrator smiled.

The Number 1 hit man loose in the Mafia jungle . . .
nothing and nobody can stop him from wiping out the
Mob!

the EXECUTIONER
by Don Pendleton

The Executioner *is without question the best-selling action/
adventure series being published today. American readers
have bought more than twenty million copies of the more
than thirty volumes published to date. Readers in England,
France, Germany, Japan, and a dozen other countries have
also become fans of Don Pendleton's peerless hero. Mack
Bolan's relentless one-man war against the Mafia, and Pendleton's unique way of mixing authenticity, the psychology of
the mission, and a bloody good story, crosses all language bar-
riers and social levels. Law enforcement officers, business executives, college students, housewives, anyone searching for a
fast-moving adventure tale, all love Bolan. It isn't just the real-
ism and violence, it certainly isn't blatant sex; it is our guess
that there is a "mystique"—if you will—that captures these
readers, an indefinable something that builds an identification
with the hero and a loyalty to the author. It must be good, it
must be better than the others to have lasted since 1969, when
War Against the Mafia, the first Executioner volume, was
published as the very first book to be printed by a newly born
company called Pinnacle Books. More than just lasting, however—as erstwhile competitors, imitators, and ripoffs died or
disappeared—The Executioner has continued to grow into an
international publishing phenomenon. The following are some
insights into the author and his hero . . . but do dare to read
any one of* The Executioner *stories, for, more than anything
else, Mack Bolan himself will convince you of his pertinence
and popularity.*

The familiar Don Pendleton byline on millions of copies of Mack Bolan's hard-hitting adventures isn't a pen name for a team of writers or some ghostly hack. Pendleton's for real ... and then some.

He had written about thirty books before he wrote the first book in *The Executioner* series. That was the start of what has now become America's hottest action series since the heyday of James Bond. With thirty-four volumes complete published in the series and four more on the drawing board, Don has little time for writing anything but *Executioner* books, answering fan mail, and autographing royalty checks.

Don completes each book in about six weeks. At the same time, he is gathering and directing the research for his next books. In addition to being a helluva storyteller, and military tactics expert, Don can just as easily speak or write about metaphysics and man's relationship to the universe.

A much-decorated veteran of World War II, Don saw action in the North Atlantic U-boat wars, the invasion of North Africa, and the assaults on Iwo Jima and Okinawa. He later led a team of naval scouts who landed in Tokyo preparatory to the Japanese surrender. As if that weren't enough, he went back for more in Korea, too!

Before turning to full-time duty at the typewriter, Don held positions as a railroad telegrapher, air traffic controller, aeronautical systems engineer, and even had a hand in the early ICBM and Moonshot programs.

He's the father of six and now makes his home in a small town in Indiana. He does his writing amidst a unique collection of weapons, photos, and books.

Most days it's just Don, his typewriter, and his dog (a German Shepherd/St. Bernard who hates strangers) sharing long hours with Mack Bolan and his relentless battle against the Mafia.

Despite little notice by literary critics, the Executioner has quietly taken his position as one of the better known, best understood, and most provocative heroes of contemporary literature—primarily through word-of-mouth advertising on the part of pleased readers.

According to Pendleton, "His saga has become identified in the minds of millions of readers as evidence (or, at least, as hope) that life is something more than some silly progression of charades through which we all drift, willy-nilly—but is a meaningful and exhilarating adventure that we all share, and to which every man and woman, regardless of situation, may contribute some meaningful dimension. Bolan is therefore considerably more than 'a light read' or momentary diversion. To the millions who expectantly 'watch' him through adventure after adventure, he has become a symbol of the revolt of institutionalized man. He is a guy *doing something*—responding to the call of his own conscience—making his presence felt in a positive sense—realizing the full potential of his own vast humanity and excellence. We are all Mack Bolan, male and female, young and old, black and white and all the shades between; down in our secret heart of hearts, where we really live, we dig the guy because *we are* the guy!

The extensive research into locale and Mafia operations that make *The Executioner* novels so lifelike and believable is always completed before the actual writing begins.

"I absorb everything I can about a particular locality, and the story sort of flows out of that. Once it starts flowing, the research phase, which may be from a couple of days to a couple of weeks, is over. I don't force the flow. Once it starts, it's all I can do to hang on."

How much of the Bolan philosophy is Don Pendleton's?

"His philosophy *is* my own," the writer insists. "Mack Bolan's struggle is a personification of the struggle of collective mankind from the dawn of time. More than that, even Bolan is a statement of the life principle—*all* life. His killing, and the motives and methods involved, is actually a consecration of the life principle. He is proclaiming, in effect, that life is meaningful, that the world is important, that it does matter what happens here, that universal goals are being shaped on this cosmic cinder called earth. That's a heroic idea. Bolan is championing the idea. That's what a hero is. Can you imagine a guy like Bolan standing calmly on the sidelines, watching without interest while a young woman is mugged and raped? The guy cares. He is reacting to a destructive principle inherent in the human situation; he's fighting it. The whole world is Bolan's family. He cares about it, and he feels that what happens to it is tremendously important. The goons have rushed in waving guns, intent on raping, looting, pillaging, destroying. And he is blowing their damned heads off, period, end of philosophy. I believe that most of *The Executioner* fans recognize and understand this rationale."

With every title in the series constantly in print and no end in sight, it seems obvious that the rapport between Don Pendleton and his legion of readers is better than ever and that the author, like his hero, has no intention of slowing down or of compromising the artistic or philosophical code of integrity that has seen him through so much.

"I don't go along with the arty, snobbish ideas about literature," he says. "I believe that the mark of good writing can be measured realistically only in terms of public response. Hemingway wrote Hemingway because he was Hemingway. Well, Pendleton writes Pendleton. I don't know any other way."

Right on, Don. Stay hard, guy. And keep those *Executioners* coming!

* * *

[Editors note: for a fascinating and incisive look into *The Executioner* and Don Pendleton, read Pinnacle's *The Executioner's War Book*, available wherever paperbacks are sold.]